Jasper & Willie
WILDFIRE

by

Bryn Fleming

D1533935

WESTWINDS
PRESS®

Library of Congress Cataloging-in-Publication Data
Fleming, Bryn.
    Jasper & Willie: wildfire / by Bryn Fleming.
        pages cm — (Range riders)
    ISBN 978-1-941821-71-8 (pbk.)
    ISBN 978-1-941821-91-6 (e-book)
    ISBN 978-1-941821-92-3 (hardbound)
    [1. Dogs—Fiction. 2. Bullying—Fiction. 3. Ranch life—Fiction. 4. People
with disabilities—Fiction.] I. Title. II. Title: Jasper and Willie: wildfire. III.
Title: Wildfire.
    PZ7.F59933Jas 2015
    [Fic]—dc23
                                2015008525

Edited by Michelle McCann
Designed by Vicki Knapton

Published by WestWinds Press®
An imprint of

GRAPHIC ARTS
BOOKS®

P.O. Box 56118
Portland, Oregon 97238-6118
503-254-5591
www.graphicartsbooks.com

"To know the least of creatures
as one of God's beings, is better
than knowing an angel."

—Meister Eckhart

Chapter 1

The second time Colton hit me, I just lay there staring up at the sky. The sun lit his head and body from behind. From the ground, he looked like an evil angel. I closed my eyes and thought that if I just kept them closed, he would disappear.

No such luck.

All I'd done was walk out the school door. Colton had grabbed me and shoved me behind the gym building. While his gang of friends, all older than me, circled around, he pounded on me.

Now Colton loomed over me, kicked the sole of my boot and said, "Hey, Gimpy, you can't run and you can't fight; what kind of a man are you?"

He turned to Ketz, his right-hand man. "He's more like a little girl, eh, Ketz?"

Ketz snickered. "Yeah, are you crying yet, little girl?" He stepped closer. If Ketz joined in pelting me I was done for. Heck, I was probably done for anyway.

"Leave me alone!" I hollered, not because I thought he'd say "Oh, okay," and go away. But I thought maybe a teacher or somebody's mom might hear. Being found on the ground like that was an embarrassing prospect but better than getting pelted some more.

I fingered my good luck horseshoe charm. Yep, still on its chain around my skinny neck, though I couldn't say it was working so good right now.

I flipped onto my side and curled up, like you'd do if a bear rolled you around in the dirt. It's supposed to make the bear lose interest, like you were already dead and your meat was going bad. Or maybe to protect your vitals from those claws. If it's a cougar after you, you stand tall and spread out your arms, looking as big as possible. I didn't reckon that'd work to scare Colton away.

Colton glared down at me. I swear little yellow flames licked out of his squinty eyes. I groaned softly, "Dios mío."

"What was that? You talkin' Spanish you little half-breed?" Colton fired off. "This is America, amigo, we speak English here!"

Colton's a big kid, even compared to the rest of his gang, so I didn't feel like telling him how stupid that sounded. Yeah, I'm half Mexican, so what?

I'm also small. That's why rolling up in a ball seemed my best option. I willed myself to shrink to nothing, to the smallest pinpoint of a target.

Colton pulled a boot back to kick me. I rolled out of reach as his foot swung by, just brushing my ribs. Don't let the bear eat you up, I said to myself.

I couldn't shrink away to nothing though, try as I

might. I was lying in the dusty school yard with my ear pressed hard into the gravel.

A dog barked in the distance. No adults in sight. The school bus hadn't pulled up yet, so the driver couldn't lean out the door and yell at the boys to stop picking on me. Teachers still straightened their desks inside. No one.

I decided my only chance was to run for it. I scrambled onto my hands and knees and jumped up. But everywhere I turned, a bigger body slid over to block my getaway.

Ketz grabbed my shoulders and shoved hard. I fell. My butt scrunched into the gravel and I yelped. The big boys started closing in. I was a rabbit surrounded by coyotes, a lamb to the slaughter. It didn't look good from my perspective.

I lowered my head and held my hands up.

"Okay, okay," my voice shook, "you win. Just stop." I thought, I won't cry. I can't cry.

Colton laughed, "Of course I win! I always win. Just like I'm going to win at football. Just like me and my dog are going to win the trials at the fair. I'm a winner, and, in case you haven't noticed, you are a loser, amigo."

A dented Ford truck came growling down from the ranch on the hill behind the school.

"Heck, it's Pa." Colton turned away from me to watch the truck.

Colton-bear was distracted by an approaching wolf, so little-rabbit-Jasper scampered for the bushes. In other words, I scrambled up and skittered in a mad dash for the shop building, the closest shelter. No one bothered to follow me; they were all staring at the road. I leaned against the cement-block wall, my heart pounding.

The rusty red truck pulled into the school lot and stopped next to the group of boys who'd been watching me get pounded a second ago. Colton rubbed his knuckles like they were sore where they'd hit my face.

A little girl, Colton's sister, probably, sat in the back of the truck, hunched up against the cab. She was scrawny and tangle-haired, maybe five or six. She gripped the side of the truck with one hand and with the other clung to a black border collie's white scruff. The dog leaned close against her, protective.

Colton stepped up and said, "Hey, Pa" through the driver's window.

Even from where I was I heard, "Just get in!" Colton walked to the passenger side, yanked open the door, and climbed in. Like a snake strike, his pa slapped the back of his head. Colton didn't even seem surprised.

Colton scowled out the window of the truck while the little girl held tight to the dog in the back. They rattled down the gravel driveway toward town, one happy little family.

When they were lost in their dust cloud, I saw Ketz catch sight of me spying around the corner of the shop building. He lunged toward me, another hungry bear looking for a snack, but I was gone before he'd taken two steps.

Chapter 2

I'm small, but fast, even if my right leg is a bit shorter than my left. I was born that way; different. Not better or worse, Mom always told me, just different. Colton used it as one more thing to jump me for. Go figure.

I didn't look back to see if Ketz or the gang was following me, I just ran.

Now, cowboy boots aren't made for running any more than a horse is made for ice-skating. I slipped and slid a couple of times before I made it down the hill. When I got to the road, I slowed down and walked. If no one offered me a ride, it'd take me about an hour and a half to reach home.

I figured I could still hustle through feeding and get the stalls forked out before my own dad got home. He was a pretty good yeller too, though it took a lot to start him up. Even at his maddest, he'd never hit me, just clenched his hands at his sides and took his anger out for a walk.

Thinking about that made me wonder about what set Colton's dad off back there. He had been red-faced and panting angry before Colton even got into the truck. Even though I still ached from Colton's beating, I didn't envy him going home with that man. Colton's pa had broken a guy's jaw once just for calling his truck a rust heap.

Maybe that's why Colton used any excuse to tackle me. Some kind of twisted revenge.

This time it had started first thing in the morning, right when Cassie got on the bus and sat down next to me, as usual. Our ranches shared a fence line on one side, so her driveway was next to mine. We were neighbors. And friends. Cassie was the first person I thought of when I had a problem: she could see an answer through the thickest dust.

On the bus, Cass and I were talking for the zillionth time about just how to convince my folks to let me have a dog. It was the only thing I wanted. The only thing missing. Mom and Dad's latest "NO!" was still echoing in my head.

Colton and his buddies filled the back of the bus with their ruckus, laughing too loud at their own stupid jokes and wrestling in the aisle until Ms. Carter caught them in her mirror. Sometimes she actually pulled the bus over and hollered, "No one's going anywhere until you boys sit down!" Like we all couldn't wait to get to school. Today she just ignored them.

Colton snickered behind us, "I can't tell which one's dressed prettier today, can you, Boxer?"

Boxer drawled, "Well, Cassie's looking fine as always, but look at Jasper's nice ironed shirt and those shiny boots."

"Hey, amigo, you stay up late polishing those things so you can look good limpin' around school?" Ketz asked me. "Where's your sombrero?"

If I was bigger and tougher I might have turned on them. I might have told them it was manly to take a pride in your appearance instead of walking around like smelly bums. But I didn't. I kept my hot face pointed front-ways. Cassie bumped my leg a couple times and rolled her eyes to make me smile.

All this was running through my head while I kicked the dust down Burnt Ranch Road as I headed home. I tasted copper pennies in my mouth—blood.

About a half mile into my walk, the crunch of tires on gravel behind me made me jump like a jackrabbit. I turned around to see who it was: Colton! I'd figured Colton and his dad were far ahead of me, but they must have stopped in town. Now that old Ford truck was rattling right for me.

The hair stood up on the back of my neck and my feet wanted to run. I told myself that Colton wouldn't dare hurt me with his pa right there. Then again . . .

I stepped off the road. Way off. I was walking in the ditch beside the road like a scaredy-cat.

The truck growled closer until I could hear it just behind me. It slowed down when they were right beside me, spitting some gravel at my leg. I glued my eyes to the dirt and kept walking. My heart pounded *thunkity-thunk* in my ears, even louder than the truck.

Colton's dad leaned across him toward the rolled-down passenger window. "Hey, kid, want a ride?"

I shook my head, but didn't look up. I didn't want to see Colton's stupid face or his dad's mean smile.

The tires dug into the gravel and the truck pulled away. When I looked up, Colton flashed me a mean grin.

The Green Canyon Ranch was just ahead. That's when it happened. Colton's dad revved up right as a jackrabbit shot across the road followed by one of the ranch dogs. The rabbit cleared the bumper and bounced off into the sagebrush.

I heard a horrible thud and a loud yelp. Then nothing.

That truck rumbled on without even slowing down. It just did a little jog around the dog and carried Colton and his pa around the bend, like nothing had happened.

I stood there frozen in shock. Holy cow! Had that just happened? Then I shook my head clear and ran to the dog lying heaped in the road. I lifted his brown and white head onto my thigh as I knelt in the dust. His body was limp, his head heavy against my leg. He was a big dog, brown and white, probably an Aussie shepherd mix, like a lot of the dogs around here. A good working dog, not a pet.

"It's going to be okay, boy," I said, even though I knew that was a lie. I sat there for a long while with his head on my lap and I thought I could feel him breathing for a bit, but then nothing. He was gone. Sounds weird, maybe, but I think I felt the moment his spirit lifted up out of him, like he got a little lighter in my arms.

I figured he must live at the Green Canyon Ranch, so I carried him up the drive. I didn't want him to lie there collecting dust and flies like roadkill. It was the least I could do.

The gravel parking area around the big ranch house was empty except for a four-wheeler with a flat tire. No truck. No car. Nobody came out the door to meet me as I carried the dead dog up the drive. I called out, "Hello? Anybody home?" Nothing.

The dog was heavy in my arms. "Deadweight" they call it, where something loses its soul and gets pulled to earth that much harder. My tears fell onto his brown fur as I lugged him up to the porch. I eased him down carefully, tucking his legs beneath him so he looked more natural. At least when his people came home they wouldn't find him on the road.

I would have left a note if I'd had paper. "Sorry about your dog. I saw who did it." And I'd have named them, too.

I looked back a couple times as I walked back down the drive. At the road, I saw the gravel messed up a bit where the dog had landed. That's all there was to mark the spot. I knew I'd think of it every time I went by.

I washed my hands in the creek beside the road. Nearby, a red-winged blackbird warbled its watery cry as it clung sideways on a cattail. A big bullfrog plopped off a half-sunken log. The afternoon sun shone bright green through the coyote willows. Far as I could tell, the world was just going along like normal. Like I hadn't been beaten sore. Like the dog was still running down the drive.

I stood and headed down the road toward home, my bum leg aching. Maybe things were normal there, too. Maybe I was the one who wasn't quite right.

Chapter 3

My thoughts rambled along with me. I knew that Colton treated his own dog poorly. In fact, I didn't know a single creature that he was kind to, unless he stood to get something out of it. It wasn't fair that he had a dog of his own and I didn't. And now this. No, sir, he didn't deserve a dog at all. Not like me.

My family had ranch dogs, cattle dogs. Everybody did here. My older brother, Danny, had his own dog, Booker. Sometimes he'd let me take Booker for walks. But now Danny was gone to college and had taken Booker with him.

I'd wanted my own dog for as long as I could remember. I wanted to choose my own pup, the one that was meant for me alone, the one who wouldn't even turn his head to anyone else's voice.

I wanted to take care of him; walk him and feed him and brush him. I'd train him to be the fastest, smartest dog in the county.

My lack of a dog hurt more than the bruises Colton gave me. Truth is I was supremely jealous of Colton. Every summer, he and his dog ran in the agility trials at the fair.

They always placed in the top three, sometimes first prize. And boy did Colton gloat over it, holding his trophy or ribbon up high and turning around in the arena like some Roman gladiator.

I don't know why I leaned against the arena rail, my stomach all knotted up, and watched them run. But I always did. And I always imagined my own dog flying around the course, over the jumps, through the tunnel, the crowd cheering us on. The judge would shout, "We have new champions, with the fastest time ever, Jasper and his dog. . . ."

It was my parents standing in the way of me and my dog, of us finally beating Colton. I'd asked them, begged them, a million times at least, starting when I was about five years old. But they had a list of reasons a mile long.

Something about seeing that dog get hit back there made me feel like I couldn't wait another day. I needed a dog now. I also needed a new angle for convincing my parents.

But what?

When I opened the door, Dad called out, "Jasper, you're late. Supper's ready." His voice came between the clatter of pans from the kitchen.

I slipped in the back door, hoping to change out of my dirty shirt and wash my face before Mom and Dad saw me. I was a sight, I'm sure: dust from the fight, fur from the dog, probably some blood too. I felt like a warrior coming home after a lost battle: achy, tired, and defeated.

"Be right there," I hollered, racing up the stairs. I'd gladly tell him and Mom about the dog, but they didn't need to know I'd gotten beat up again. They'd just worry about me, like last time. They might even want to call Colton's dad. What a disaster *that* would be!

In the bathroom, water swirled dirty brown in the sink as I scrubbed my face and dabbed at the gravel scrapes on my arms. I put on a clean button-down shirt and rolled down the sleeves to hide the cuts and the purple-brown bruises starting to blossom. I ran my fingers through my mess of black hair, then went downstairs and plopped into my chair, trying to look normal.

When we were all sitting with our heads bowed, Mom said grace, asking blessings on the ranch and the family.

"Amen," I said and really meant it. I could use some blessing right now.

Mom stabbed her steak and Dad passed the corn around. I dished potatoes and green beans onto my plate and kept my head down. My stomach churned like a concrete mixer as I shoved my food around. When I looked up, both of them were staring at me.

"You're too quiet, Jasper. Something happen today?" Mom asked.

I got that fear-relief combo punch in my gut. No avoiding it. I started talking, still staring at my green beans.

"I missed the bus today and had to walk home and when I got to the Green Canyon Ranch, Colton and his dad drove by me in their truck and then this dog that was chasing a jackrabbit ran out onto the road and they hit it. The dog, not the rabbit," I blurted.

"What?" my mom gasped, her fork frozen in midair.

"It was a horrible sound. Thud . . . or thump. And he yelped. But they just kept going." I sucked in my breath.

"That's terrible!" Mom put her fork down.

"I picked him up." Feeling the limp dog in my arms again, a couple tears got away from me and rolled down my cheeks. "He was so heavy, so . . . dead. I carried him up to the house. But no one was home, so I left him on the porch. I just couldn't leave him lying in the road."

"They didn't even stop?" Dad asked, his forehead all furrowed up and his eyes narrowed.

"Nope."

Dad shook his head. He reached over the corner of the table and awkwardly patted my shoulder. "You did the right thing, son."

"Someone needs to teach those folks some respect." Mom's face flushed red. "I'd like to be the one to do it." Mom wasn't afraid of anybody.

"You can't make people do right." Dad chewed his steak slowly. "Best to avoid the troublemakers. They're not worth your time."

"That's for sure," I said, running my fork through the mashed potatoes. But sometimes trouble won't be ignored.

Dad said, "I'll let Mr. Dinapoli over at Green Canyon know what happened. "Or," he paused a second, "would you like to call them yourself?"

It was the grown-up thing to do. A boy old enough to have his own dog would do it.

"I'll call after dinner," I said, even though I was scared to tell what I'd seen. If Colton heard that I'd told, I'd get another beating. Maybe his dad would even kill me if he got in trouble with the law over it.

My dad nodded, his eyebrows raised, like he was surprised to hear it. Mom just nodded. I jumped on it while they were admiring how grown up I was:

"I swear if I had my own dog, I'd never let it run out in the road and get hurt."

"We know you wouldn't, son," Dad said. He paused like there might be a tiny light of possibility. I held my breath. Then he said, "But . . ."

Here it comes.

". . . we have plenty of animals to take care of as it is. You've got school all day, and your mom and I keep busy with the cattle."

"Also," Mom added, "a dog isn't cheap to feed, and then there are the vet bills."

Dad took another turn: "An animal on a ranch has to be of use. Either it has a job to do or it's something we can eat."

Same old arguments: Time and money.

But my parents were just plain wrong. Somehow, and soon, I'd get my dog.

Chapter 4

By the time dinner was finished, I was tired all over, and not the good kind of tired from working all day. I took my time wiping the sudsy warm water over the dishes and rinsing each fork and spoon and plate.

When I'd hung the last clean mug on its hook, I went to the living room to make the call to tell Mr. Dinapoli about how his dog got killed.

"Hello? Mr. Dinapoli?" My words cracked and shook.

The gravelly voice on the line said, "Yes?"

"This is Jasper, from down the road."

"Yes?" he said again.

Then I just wanted to get it all out. "I'm sorry about your dog. I was walking home and a truck ran into him. I put him on the porch, but he was dead already."

"Thanks, Jasper," Mr. Dinapoli went silent for a minute. "Did you see who did it?"

I swallowed hard. "No sir, I didn't. They were going fast. They didn't stop."

He growled some swearwords and said, "Thank you, Jasper. I was mighty fond of Rudy. He was a good cow dog."

I could hear sadness in his voice now, a low slowness, mixed with his anger.

"Sorry again." I said, "Bye," and hung up. I hadn't told on Colton. What a chicken I was.

My whole body ached and dinner sat like a lump in my stomach. I had to talk to Cassie. She knows me better than anyone. I knew I wouldn't sleep until I talked to her, told her how I'd failed.

"Mom, can I go to Cassie's for a little bit?"

Dad had gone out to feed the stock horses. Mom was at the dining room table, sorting through the mail.

"Dishes done?"

"Yep, I said, "done and put away."

"Be home by dark," I heard behind me as I thudded out the screen door.

My horse, Tigger, trotted up to the pasture gate. I rubbed her smooth tan nose and the velvet behind her black-rimmed ears. She nuzzled my shirt pocket, looking for a peppermint. "Sorry, girl, I forgot to grab one."

I got Tig's halter out of the barn and caught her up and tied her to the fence rail. I brushed her dun coat and ran a comb through her black mane, but didn't bother with her tail. I lifted each hoof to check for rocks and picked a chunk of gravel out of her left front.

I shook out her saddle pad, a red and black and white Mexican blanket folded in half, laid it forward, up on her withers, and then slid it back so the hair was smooth and flat underneath. I snugged the cinch up tight and finger-combed the strands of black forelock that liked to tangle under her bridle.

I tucked my left foot into the stirrup, grabbed the saddle horn, and swung up.

We headed out the old wagon road, clip-clopping slowly into the oncoming dusk. I looked behind me a couple times, imagining a dog trotting at Tig's heel.

I even gave a short whistle and said, "Come on, boy, keep up." If I had my own dog he'd believe in me no matter what I said or did, no matter how cowardly I was.

When I topped the rise, I saw Cassie dumping a wheelbarrow of straw and manure onto the big pile in the barnyard.

Cassie was as hard a worker as any kid I knew, especially since it was just her and her dad and her sister, Fran. She could do anything from fixing fence to welding water tanks. She could definitely beat me at arm wrestling.

Cassie was in my grade but a head taller than me. She had blue eyes instead of brown, like mine, and long brown hair she tied back in a pony tail. We've been friends since we rescued a horse together. She glanced up at me and waved.

"Hey," I said when Tig and I got to the bottom of the hill, "almost done?"

"Hey." She tipped the wheelbarrow and gave it a kick to roll the last horse manure out. "Yep, one more stall."

I tied Tig to the hitching rail and followed Cassie into the warm, dark shadows of the barn. Little bits of dust floated in the light.

"I'll do it," I grabbed the pitchfork from against the wall. I was avoiding my confession, even though that's what I'd come for.

She led her paint horse, Rowdy, into the hallway between the stalls and held his lead rope while I forked the wet straw and manure into the wheelbarrow. The ammonia smell of horse pee stung my eyes.

"Where'd you go after school?" I asked her.

"Dentist appointment. Pa picked me up early." I liked Cassie's dad. Her big sister, Fran, not so much. Since their mom had passed away, Fran, who was fifteen, had decided she was boss now.

"Well," I said, "you missed a couple things."

I rolled up my sleeves to show the gravel skids on my arms. "Colton and Ketz and their gang of morons tackled me."

"That doesn't sound like a fair fight." She looked me up and down, checking out the damage.

Cassie shook her head, put Rowdy back in his stall, and followed me while I pushed the wheelbarrow back out to the pile and dumped it. "I don't suppose you got any punches in?"

She wasn't trying to be ornery, just realistic.

"Not really," I said.

I upended the wheelbarrow against the barn where I knew they kept it and parked the pitchfork next to it. Climbed up on the top rail of the corral. I was still stalling. Cassie sprang up next to me.

The crickets started up, chirping into the silence

between us. Cassie reached over and flicked the brim of my black cowboy hat playfully. "What else?" Yep, she knew me.

I couldn't put it off anymore; I told her about Colton's dad hitting Rudy with the truck, them just driving away and Colton grinning out the window like a demon.

"And, to top off the day," I added, "Mom and Dad still won't let me have a dog. I thought they might be softened up, you know, after Rudy, but no."

But I couldn't get the rest of words out, how I'd lied about not seeing who'd hit the dog. I was a double-chicken, afraid to tell Mr. D. and now afraid to tell my best friend. I hung my head.

"That stinks," she said. "Colton needs to get what's coming to him."

Rowdy whinnied from his stall in the barn.

"He smells the wildfires," Cassie said, "even though they're miles away."

Cassie hopped off the rail and wiped her hands on the butt of her jeans.

"You'll get your dog," she said. "I'll think of something. Now, let's go for a ride and check out the fire."

My dad always quotes somebody or other and says that there's nothing better for the inside of a man than the outside of a horse. I reckon that's true, because a fast ride on a good horse can really clear a guy's head.

"Yeah, okay." I jumped down and untied Tig, glad to be moving and not just talking.

Chapter 5

C assie haltered Rowdy and led him from his stall. He nibbled some hay from the floor while she got his bridle. He blinked his blue eyes at her and rubbed his long white nose against her shirt. She slipped the bridle over his head and buckled the cheek strap, straightening his forelock over the brow band.

"Give me a leg up, I'm going bareback," she said.

I laced my fingers together like a stirrup and she put her foot in and I lifted a little while she swung up onto Rowdy's back. I barely had my own foot in the stirrup when she and Rowdy shot off.

We raced Tig and Rowdy up and over the hill to the east, the one that bordered the public lands. Both horses liked to canter uphill, easier than plodding up at a walk, so we ate up the slope in big reaching strides. Cassie and Rowdy skidded to a stop when they crested the rise. Tig and I caught up.

The John Day River Valley spread out below us, the river itself winding east to west. Sagebrush flats sloped up to juniper-dotted hills and then to rimrock cliffs. Sutton Mountain loomed in the east, miles long and flat-topped.

"Wow! Look at that!" Cassie pointed toward Sutton.

Yellow and orange wildfire lit the north end of the peak, from the rocky rim down over the hunched shoulder. Black smoke billowed up and turned the white clouds dusky gray.

Wildfires are part of life out here; lightning cracks a tree snag in two or a guy tosses a cigarette butt out the truck window. They burn thousands of acres a year, racing through the sage and juniper or up into the lodgepole pines on the mountain slopes.

On the flats, the fires eat up grassland. Ranchers worry when grazing gets scarce for the cattle and when fences and barns burn up. But up in the mountains, the fires clear out the dead wood and underbrush; less fuel means smaller fires, which are easier to control.

"It's early for wildfire season to start," I ventured. "You don't usually see a fire that big until August or September."

"Well, last year was dry," Cassie reminded me. "Hardly any snow, no fall rain, barely any in the spring, even. Pa says wildfires will be bad this summer."

"It's kind of scary, how quick the sage and juniper burn." I'd helped dig a fire line around my uncle's house last summer, when sparks from his welder lit fire to the hillside outside the shop. The heat from the flames, the charred ground and smoking stumps burned in my memory, and the way the flames licked across the dirt where there seemed to be nothing to burn.

I slipped my boots out of my stirrups and dangled my

feet. Tig tore at the bunchgrass and chewed it slowly, uncon-cerned about the distant smoke and flames. Rowdy jigged and snorted, flaring his nostrils to smell if the fire was a danger to us.

"There's something else I didn't tell you," I said into the smoky air. "When I called and told Mr. D. about Rudy, I lied and said I didn't see who did it."

Cassie looked at me hard. "Really?" she said. "You missed a chance to rat on Colton?"

I couldn't look her in the eye, but gazed off at the grow-ing smoke plume in the distance. "I was scared."

We sat in silence for another minute. I squirmed in the saddle and swung my feet. I couldn't tell if she was thinking that I was a scaredy-cat or if she would have done the same.

"I swear, we're going to get back at Colton," Cassie finally said.

I looked up at my friend. She understood. It was her and me against the bully.

"I have an idea," she said. "How about if we train your dog for the agility trials? Then we could beat Colton and Fencer at the fair next summer."

"You read my mind! Could we really do it?"

"Of course!" she said, like it was the most natural thing in the world for us to beat Colton at his own game. "We just need the right dog: a smart dog with fast feet."

I caught her spark and grinned. "Yeah, we can train him ourselves. Look at how you trained Rowdy to run bar-rels for the rodeo. You guys are amazing. I can't wait to see the look on Colton's face when me and my dog win the agility trophy at the fair."

Cassie went on, "We'll build a course with jumps and tunnels and everything. Then we'll practice every day after school until he's the best and the fastest. . . ."

I could picture it all in my mind, me running alongside my dog, urging him on; him all sleek and focused, running from one obstacle to the next, fast as lightning, fast as wildfire across the plains. Cassie at the rail cheering for us.

Cassie knew animals inside and out. I'd seen her train the toughest horses, all with gentleness and a firm hand. I had no doubt that she could make any dog into a champion.

"But, how are we gonna get my folks to give in and let me have a dog?" I asked. "Nothing I've tried has worked. They want me to wait *years!*"

Cassie thought a minute. "The best way to make something happen is to get ready for it, like it's already for certain. So, we need to get all ready for your dog, build a doghouse, buy a collar and food and everything."

I must have looked doubtful, but she just kept going, "You can get a job and save the money to take care of him."

I thought it over, running my fingers through Tig's mane. "I think you're right, Cass. I think it just might work."

"You bet it will work. You'll have to tell your folks about the job. Can't hide that. But we can build the doghouse and training course in secret. Right up until we're done."

"Why's that?"

Cassie turned Rowdy back toward home. Over her shoulder, she said, "So we can show your folks all at once how serious you are. Then they won't be able to say 'no'."

"Come on," she hollered, nudging Rowdy up into a canter and letting out a war whoop to wake the dead.

Tig and I galloped after her.

Chapter 6

Smoky air drifted around the house that night, seeping into my dreams: I was scrunched down in my sleeping bag next to a campfire, the wood crackling and sparking, the sparks lifting into the night sky. . . .

"Jasper!"

I jerked awake, groggy and confused. I heard an engine rev in the driveway and the front door squeal open then bang shut. My clock glowed green: 5:30.

"Jaaaasper!"

I scrambled into my jeans. "Coming, Dad!"

When I hit the bottom of the stairs, Dad was lacing up his work boots in the hall.

"The fire's jumped the road down by Fosters. We're going to help keep it off the house and barn."

My heart was beating a million miles an hour as we sped off into the smoky night. We turned off Burnt Ranch onto the access road and headed toward Sutton Mountain. Sunrise lit the sky deep red in the east and a huge plume of rosy pink smoke lifted up off the north ridge of the mountain, right above Foster's place.

My heart raced and my mouth was dry. I was scared and excited at once.

As we got closer, I could see the actual fire, not just smoke: licks of flame shot off the tops of junipers. Where the trees were close enough together, the flames reached out like arms and jumped from one treetop to another. Sure felt like we should be running away from the fire instead of going toward it. . . . But neighbors help neighbors. They'd do the same for us if the fire was roaring toward *our* ranch.

We skidded to a stop next to five or six other trucks and hopped out. "Thanks for coming, everybody." I hardly recognized Mr. Foster, his jeans and T-shirt dusty gray and streaked with black, his hair greasy and mussed.

Our neighbors looked different, too, in the smoky night, like ghosts of themselves. I didn't see Cassie or Fran or their dad.

"The fire's jumped the road at the east fence line," Mr. Foster said. "If it keeps coming on, the house and barns will burn."

He went on, "We need to make a fire line between the ranch buildings and the fire—a bare strip of ground about five feet wide. When the fire hits bare dirt, it'll have nothing to burn and it'll die out."

"Jasper and I can start south and work up," Dad said. We had our orders. Time to fight the fire.

I jumped back into the bed of our truck and a guy I didn't know got up front with Dad. Toby, a kid from school a couple years ahead of me, climbed in back with me. I hoped he didn't notice me shaking.

I stood looking over the cab, shovels rattling at my feet, smoky wind in my face. That's when I saw Colton.

His dad's truck sped up the drive and wheeled in tight behind us. Just what I needed; something else to worry about. What if he got a hold of me out in the smoke with the fire bearing down on us?

When I could hear the sparks and feel the heat of the fire raging ahead of us, Dad stopped and Toby and I grabbed shovels and jumped down. Colton and his dad parked behind us.

"Stay!" Colton hollered and I saw Fencer crouch down in the bed of the truck. Why in the world would Colton bring his dog to a wildfire? I'd never put *my* dog in danger! Colton raised his hand and Fencer cowered against the cab. And I wouldn't train *my* dog with fear either.

Colton saw me watching him. "Don't touch my dog," he growled over his shoulder and disappeared into the smoke.

We all spread out in a line across the rocky ground. The fire crackled and sparked through clumps of sage, sizzled through the bunchgrass. I dug hard and fast, hacking at sage clumps, panting as I threw shovel after shovel of gravelly dirt aside.

For a while, Colton dug just a few feet away from me. I kept my eyes on the ground in front of me.

My back ached. My arms ached. My short leg throbbed.

I was hot and sore all over. I guess an hour or so flew by; it was hard to tell, like the smoke blurred time.

Suddenly, a big stand of junipers exploded a few yards ahead, showering sparks down on me. I covered my eyes with my arm. Smoke and flames roared skyward like fireworks.

I saw a low dark movement off to my left, between me and the leaping flames. A coyote? A fox? There were probably dozens of animals running ahead of the fire, trying to escape. The animal paused and looked right at me. Black with a white ruff. Not a coyote, a dog. Fencer!

Fencer was running every which way, crazy and scared, confused by the smoke and the roar of the fire. Then he ran *toward* the flames instead of away.

"No, Fencer!" I yelled. "Get back!" My heart leaped. He was heading straight into the burning brush.

I'm no hero. I could have peed my pants I was so scared as I sprinted toward the fire, hoping to head Fencer off.

When I got close, the heat from the flames scorched my cheeks, hot as a horseshoe out of a blacksmith's fire. I stretched out my hand. "Come here, Fencer. Here boy."

When I was just a couple feet from the scared dog, I lunged for him. I snagged his collar tight and pulled him toward me.

He thrashed in my arms as I stumbled toward where I thought the trucks should be. He was a big dog and heavy and wrenched himself this way and that. He had no idea I was trying to help him.

I turned in circles, squinting through the smoke. Where were the trucks? Where was Dad? My eyes burned; tears blurred everything. Fencer struggled harder in my arms. Then I tripped over a rock. I couldn't break my fall without letting go of Fencer. I landed on my side, my cheek in the dirt, my forehead against a rock. Fencer squirmed out of my arms while I lay there, dazed.

I struggled up to my knees. A hand came out of nowhere. I'd been peering into the smoke so hard looking for Fencer I hadn't noticed my dad come up behind me.

"Come on, Jasper!" He shouted over the crackling of the fire. "Let's get back to the truck!"

Dad pulled me to my feet and we stumbled through the smoke. I sat down on the tailgate, exhausted. I guess I'd scraped my face when I fell, because Dad wiped a trickle of blood from my cheek.

"Jasper," Dad took hold of my shoulders. "You okay?"

My throat hurt when I tried to talk. "Where's Fencer?"

"Where's what?" Dad asked.

"Colton's dog, where is he?"

"Oh. He's over there in the truck." Dad pointed.

I stood up. There was Fencer, crouched and panting in the back of Colton's dad's truck. He'd found his way back. My legs buckled and I sat back down on the tailgate, coughing.

Dad's face was soft and worried. "When that stand of trees exploded I looked up and you were gone in the smoke."

"Sorry."

Dad shook his head. "I should have kept better track of you."

"I'm okay." I was embarrassed. I didn't want my dad to babysit me. I wanted to be a man fighting fire. "Can we keep digging? I'm okay now, really." I stood up and my head spun.

"No need," Mr. Foster said. "After those junipers went, the fire hit our line and burned back on itself."

Sure enough, the flames were already dying down. They'd eaten everything in their path and come up against the fire line we'd dug. On the other side of the line, bunchgrass sizzled and embers glowed in the stumps of junipers. The ground was black. On this side, the ground was untouched, dried grass unburned, sagebrush dusky green.

Mr. Foster thanked us all and shook everybody's hands, even mine, even though I'd fallen and had to get pulled out.

Sometime on the ride home, I decided it was okay that nobody knew about how I'd probably saved Fencer's life. I'd tell Cassie, of course, but no one else. Maybe a good deed was an even better thing if no one knew you'd done it.

Mom met us at the door. She gently prodded the bump on my head while Dad told her what had happened. Once she finally decided I was okay, I dragged myself upstairs to wash off the soot and dirt.

It was a school day, a regular old day, despite what I'd been through. I splashed water on my face and imagined telling Cassie about the fire and about Fencer, too.

Dad stuck his head around the bathroom door. "You

did a good job out there, son. I was proud to work with you."

He hardly ever said stuff like that. I scrubbed my face with a towel, embarrassed. "Thanks, Dad," I mumbled through the cloth.

"When you're washed up, you go back to bed, Jasper. I'll call the school and tell them you need to rest."

"But . . ." I started, then quit. I took my achy self to my room and fell onto the bed.

Lying there safe and sound, the whole thing ran through my head. If I'd let Fencer run into the fire, Colton wouldn't win the agility trials. But I could never do that. It wasn't Fencer's fault that Colton was a jerk. I thought about my own dog, the one I'd always keep safe.

I smiled to myself. I'd fought a fire, even though I was afraid. I'd gone after a dog in trouble, gone right into danger to rescue him.

Maybe I wasn't such a chicken after all.

Chapter 7

When I opened my eyes again it was 2:14. Yellow light streamed between the shade and the windowsill. Afternoon. I sat up.

My head throbbed in time with a rapping on my door. "Yeah?" I grumbled, sleepy and hurting.

Mom poked her head around. "I brought you some breakfast . . . well, lunch."

I moved a pile of books and she set the tray on the nightstand. A ham sandwich and a scoop of potato salad. And a big glass of ice water that I grabbed and slugged down in two seconds.

"You're dehydrated," Mom said. "Head hurt?"

I nodded. "Oh yeah."

She nodded. "All that sweating and the heat. I'll get you more water."

I sat back against the headboard, chewing the sandwich, still smelling the smoke in my hair, in the pile of clothes I'd left on the floor. I rubbed the big bump on my forehead. For a firefighting, dog-saving hero, I was in sorry shape. Heck, the scrapes from my fight with Colton still hurt.

You know what would make me feel better right now? I thought. A dog of my own! I could practically picture him, curled up on the bed next to me. I would reach out to scratch behind his ears and he would thump his tail happily, then gaze up at me with concern. Maybe lick my hand.

When Mom came back with more water, I said, "You know, I could get one of those firefighting dogs—a Dalmatian." Couldn't hurt to try while she was feeling all tender toward me. "I could name him Sparky or Smoky."

Mom ran her fingers through my hair like she hadn't done since I was ten or so. "I'll think about it," she said.

What? A spark in the night! She didn't say "no"!

I finished eating and practically skipped to the bathroom, the tiredness and pain suddenly lifting. Then I saw myself in the mirror: Dios mío! I looked awful! Blue-black bags under my eyes, hair like a bird's nest, and a golf ball–sized lump on my forehead. But I grinned at my reflection anyway, my insides doing a loop like on a roller coaster: Mom had practically said yes! I did a little jig around the bathroom. My dog was getting closer every day!

The hours dragged by until I knew Cassie would be home from school. I tried to read, tried to rest, tried to *not* think about the fire and Fencer and my own dog. Mostly I just stared out the window.

Cassie picked up on the second ring and immediately blurted, "Jas, Toby told me all about the fire, how you almost died and how your dad had to rescue you. What happened?"

Great. Toby stole my surprise. But I told her all about it anyway, trying to make myself sound a little less sorry and a lot more brave.

"Colton brought Fencer to the fire. Can you believe it?" I told her how I ran after the dog, almost right into the fire.

"That's amazing! What did Colton say when he found out you saved his dog?"

"Well," I didn't know how to put it into words. "I didn't tell him. I didn't really tell anybody."

"Why not? Why wouldn't you. . . ."

"I don't know. I . . . Can we drop it, please?"

"Yeah, fine." She went on, "I wanted to go fight the fire, too, but Pa's selling a load of cows in Reno, so it's just Fran and me. She'd never have let me go."

"I figured something like that when I didn't see you."

"School wasn't too bad today." Cassie said. "You missed a biology test. I actually did okay. Can you believe it?"

Cassie was never a big fan of school, but she'd been trying harder this year, well, ever since we rescued the horse. Ever since she decided her education might *actually be* important.

"Anyway," she said, "you should read chapter 5 and 6. Do you have your biology book or do you need me to bring mine over?"

"Wow, you *actually* brought your book home? *After* the test even?"

"Yeah, yeah, I'm a real nerd now. Do you need it or not?"

My stack of schoolbooks sat on the chair, right where I'd left them two days ago. "No, I'm good. I'll study tonight."

I changed the subject: "You know how you said I should get ready for my dog, just like he's really coming?"

"Yeah."

"Well, I think Mom's coming around to the idea. Will you help me build a doghouse next weekend?"

"Sure."

"And I need to start saving money for my dog fund," I added. "I need a job." My head was working overtime now, thinking more about the dog than about the fire or what I'd missed at school.

"All right, we'd better get to work then. What kind of a job do you think you can get?"

"I could check at the general store, see if they need somebody to clean up and stock shelves."

"Maybe," Cassie sounded doubtful. "That's really a family business. I've never seen them hire anybody who wasn't related."

"How about the feed store? I could load bags of feed and stack hay bales."

"You should go ask them after school," Cassie said. "And odd jobs, mowing yards in town, fixing fence. Later this summer you could help with the haying. You can drive a baler, right?"

"I can drive our tractor. Can't be much different."

"Let's put up a sign at the post office: 'Hard Worker willing to do just about anything to get a dog'."

"Yeah, right." I laughed. "I'll go around to the neighbors after I ask at the feed store."

"It'll all come together, you'll see. Pretty soon you'll be working twenty-four hours a day, no time for school or chores and with money coming out your ears. You can get a whole pack of dogs!"

"One good dog will do me just fine."

Good old Cassie. I smiled when I hung up the phone. She always knew how to turn my day around.

Tomorrow I'd go to every business in town after school. *Somebody* had to hire me.

I imagined myself counting up my dog money. I found an old cigar box to keep it in and wrote "Dog Fund" on it with a black felt tip pen. I felt like I was closer than ever to getting my dog.

Chapter 8

The next morning after breakfast I scoured the "Help Wanted" section of the paper. Nothing for an almost-twelve-year-old.

School dragged by. Only the biology test was halfway exciting and that was only because I hadn't studied for it at all. My mind had been full of plans and ideas that had nothing to do with biology.

Instead of taking the bus home, I walked down to the feed store on Main Street. Cassie had to go home, so I didn't have her for moral support.

A handful of businesses sat scattered along the street; a general store, the post office, two cafes, a what-not shop with junk and antiques for the tourists, an old hotel that was haunted by a little girl named "Patty" (but that's another story), the feed store, and a tire store.

I stopped in the general store first, the "Merc" (for mercantile) my folks called it. They carried a little bit of everything. The building was about a hundred years old, weathered wood with a wide porch where the owner, Mr. Bailey, sat in the summer.

Mr. Bailey sat behind the cash register reading *Field and Stream*. He looked over his half-glasses. "Hello, Jasper," he said as the harness bells above the door jangled. "What brings you by? Mom run out of chain-saw oil again?" He put his magazine on the counter.

The heads of different animals stared down on me from the walls; a glassy-eyed buck deer, an elk as big as a horse, and a huge hairy wild boar that Mr. Bailey had shot on a hunting trip to California.

"No, thanks, Mr. B. Just looking." All of a sudden I felt shy and nervous. What if he laughed at me for thinking I was old enough to have a job? I almost turned around and left. Then I thought of my dog.

I walked back to the cooler, took out a pop and then put it back. Went to the candy rack and picked up a chocolate bar, changed it for a pack of gum, then put that back.

"Can I help you find something?" Mr. Bailey asked.

"Well," I stepped up to the counter and let out the breath I'd been holding. "I wondered if you need any help around here, cleaning up or putting things on the shelf or anything."

It only had five short aisles and freezers and coolers around the edges. There were bins of nails and nuts and bolts across the back wall and half an aisle of rubber boots, gloves, and hats. The rest was canned goods, bread, cookies, and such.

He shook his head. "Sorry, Jasper, I think Mrs. Bailey and I have everything under control here."

"Um, okay," I turned to go. "You know anybody might need a hard worker?"

"Not off the top of my head." He scratched his head, like that helped the ideas come out. "I'll keep you in mind, though, if I hear of anything."

"Okay, thanks." I dodged out the door, letting it bang and jangle behind me. It was harder than I thought to ask for work. Maybe no one would hire me and I'd never earn any money and I'd never get my dog.

Cassie's voice came into my head then, telling me that everything would work out, that I'd get my dog and we'd beat Colton and Fencer at the fair. I decided I'd just keep asking until I found my job, no matter how many places I had to go and how many times I heard "No."

And that's pretty much how it went for the rest of the afternoon; "No" at the feed store, "No" at the tire store, even "No, sorry," at both cafes and a "maybe you can mow the lawn next week" at the hotel.

All afternoon just for one possible lawn-mowing job and now I had a long walk home and probably a lecture for being late at my chores.

I made one last stop on the walk out of town: the post office. I knew there was no job for me there, but maybe there'd be something on the bulletin board where everybody put up signs from "FRESH EGGS $2.00 A DOZEN" to "Men's Bible Study Friday Night, 7:00 PM, Baptist Church."

I scanned the typed and handwritten notices. There it was:

HELP WANTED
HARD WORKERS TO MOVE IRRIGATION PIPE
MORNINGS AND WEEKENDS
APPLY AT THE FLYING M RANCH

My heart jumped in my chest. I felt like the job had appeared just for me. I almost ripped the notice down to take with me, I was so excited. Instead, I dashed out the door, jumped down the three steps to the sidewalk and whooped, punching the air.

I ran almost all the way home, which is *miles*, so you can see how happy I was.

I knew that moving irrigation pipe was hard work. The wheel lines held the pipes off the ground about three feet. The sprinklers sprayed out of the tops of the pipes every few yards. Each "wheel line" needed to be moved across the pasture a couple times a day by rolling the big wheels forward, so that the sprinklers watered the whole field. A few ranches had motors that moved the wheels, but a lot of them still had to be moved by hand.

I pictured myself working alongside the high schoolers, who usually took the few ranch jobs that opened up around here. I could push the giant metal wheels that held the sprinkler pipe as well as any bigger kid. I'd get there early and never take breaks and come home with my pockets full of money for my Dog Fund.

Chapter 9

The next Saturday, after breakfast and chores, I saddled Tig up. She tossed her head and danced around while I tried to get my foot in the stirrup.

"Feeling feisty, huh? Well, cut it out, buddy; this is important." I gave her a little slap on the neck and she crow-hopped to show me what she thought of my important errand. It would take about a half hour to ride to the hay ranch to apply for the job.

I trotted her down the driveway and out onto the paved road. We turned on Skyline Road. It was probably four or five miles to the Flying M. The sun was well up and passing behind some nice white clouds.

Coming around the north end of Sutton Mountain, the whole huge ranch spread out like a patchwork quilt over the valley; plowed fields furrowed brown, yellow-brown stubble fields still fallow from last year, green pasture dotted with black cattle. All this lay crisscrossed by fences and dirt roads.

Two tall posts held a weathered sign over the driveway: "Flying M Ranch." This was it. My heart beat faster as I rode Tig under the sign and up the drive toward the main house and my new job, I hoped. The house sat in its green grass yard, shade trees arched over it, a cluster of barns, sheds, and corrals around it and a neat split-rail fence around that.

I tied Tig to the top rail of the corral closest to the house. She reached down and tore off a big mouthful of the soft green lawn. It took a lot of water, and money, to keep things so lush and green out here in sagebrush country. The ranch must be doing really well.

The log house was one story, but sprawling, like it had been added to as the family got bigger. A dog barked inside the house as I clumped up the steps. I rubbed my horseshoe charm, took a big breath, and knocked at the door.

When Mr. McPheeter opened the door, I couldn't talk for a minute. I'd seen him towering over my dad when they talked at the auction yard a few times, but he looked like a giant as he stood there taking up the whole doorway.

"Yes?" I think he said it twice before I gathered up enough courage to speak.

"I'd like a job moving irrigation pipe, sir," I said. Then I remembered my manners. I took off my black felt cowboy hat and added, "I'm Jasper from over on Burnt Ranch and I want to buy a dog so I need a job."

"Well, Jasper from over on Burnt Ranch, how old are you?"

It was the question I was afraid he'd ask. But I held my head up. "I'm twelve, sir. But I'm plenty strong and very reliable, and. . . ." I thought about it for a second, "And I'm highly motivated, sir."

He laughed and stood back and looked me over. "I don't think so, Jasper. It's heavy work." He started to back out of the doorway. "Maybe when you're older."

I knew he meant, "Maybe when you're bigger and stronger." So I spoke up. "I know I'm kind of small, but I'm really strong. And I'll be on time every day and I won't quit early or take breaks or anything."

He stepped back into the doorway and looked me over from head to toe and back again.

My stomach turned and knotted as I stood there, my heart pounding in my chest; what if he didn't hire me after all? I'd ride home without a job, without a way to make money for my dog. I'd have to tell Cassie. . . .

Finally, he said, "All right, I'll give you a try. But if you can't keep up, you're out. Clear?"

"Yes, sir!" I grinned. I wanted to jump up in the air and holler, but that would have to wait. Right now, I was almost an adult getting hired for an important job. I smiled like I'd just ridden the biggest, meanest bull at the rodeo. "Yes, sir, I understand. You won't be sorry."

"You start Monday at six. That's six in the morning. You'll work Monday through Friday starting at six and Saturday you can start at eight. My regular hired hands will take care of Sunday."

"Yes, sir," I said. I wanted to ask how much money I'd make but didn't know if I should. . . .

He went on, like he'd read my mind: "You'll be done by eight on weekdays. That's two hours a day, six days a week, twenty dollars a day. Payday is after work Saturday."

I tried to figure out in my head how many weeks I'd have to work before I could afford a dog, but came up blank. I'd work it out on the way home. Anyway, I'd have my dog soon!

He added, "If it doesn't rain, we'll be watering for five or six weeks on the first crop. I may need you again later in the summer. We'll see how you do." He looked me up and down again. "Don't be late, because there are plenty of older kids who'd be happy to take your place."

"Yes, sir, thank you!" I remembered I was going to do a man's job and turned back and put out my hand. It disappeared in his giant paw. He was chuckling as he closed the door, but I didn't care.

I had a job! I was closer than ever to getting my dog.

I untied Tig, swung up, and we walked back toward home. It was a nice warm afternoon and I was glad to be out riding and thinking. I rehearsed how I'd tell my parents about my new job when I got home, straight out, not like I was asking if I could.

As we finished up dinner that evening, Mom was sipping her coffee and I waited until Dad was wiping his mouth with his yellow cloth napkin, pushing his chair back from the table.

I decided to dive right in. "I got a job today, moving pipe at the Flying M. So I can pay for my own dog."

That kind of stopped the small talk for a minute while they both looked at me.

"I start on Monday at 6:00 A.M."

Dad looked over at Mom. She was shaking her head and Dad had a steely, determined look to his eyes.

"No." Mom said it straight, just like I had.

"I agree, son, it's too much and too early. Your schoolwork would suffer and what about your chores?"

I guess they didn't realize that I wasn't the same young kid I'd been a few weeks ago, before I decided to make this happen, to get a dog no matter what it took. I was prepared.

"Why not let me try at least?" I bargained. "If I get behind at school, at all, I'll quit. I promise. And I'll make sure Tig's fed before I go to work and I'll do extra chores after school if you want." I waited. "Please. It's important."

More silence.

Mom spoke first. "I guess we could let you try, if your dad agrees. Honey? What do you think?"

"You're showing a lot of initiative, Jasper. I appreciate that. And you're certainly persistent." He smiled. "Okay. But that doesn't mean we're agreeing to the dog. We'll have to see how this job goes, first."

I hugged Mom and shook Dad's hand, just like I'd done with Mr. McPheeter. I felt ten feet tall. It was all I could do not to jump and holler.

"You can't ride Tigger out there in the dark," Dad said. "Better be ready at 5:45. I'll give you a lift."

I grinned. "I'll make the coffee."

I dialed Cassie's number a split second after I had the last plate stashed in the cupboard.

"Guess what?"

"Hmm, let me see. . . ." she teased.

Before she could get in another word, I hollered, "I got the job!" And told her all about it.

"That's great, Jas! So, if you're starting Monday, we better get to work on the doghouse tomorrow."

"All right. Meet me over here after chores?"

"I'll be there," and she hung up.

I whistled while I fed Tig and made sure the chickens were safe in their coop. That was something else my dog could help with, keeping skunks and raccoons and foxes out of the chicken pen.

I went to bed happier than I'd been for a long time. I could almost feel the weight of my dog on the end of the bed.

Chapter 10

Cassie was true to her word. She rode up on Rowdy just as I was finishing my chores. The water troughs were all full, the cows were fed, Tig was munching her grain in the corral.

Sunday morning: time to build the doghouse.

"You can put Rowdy in the corral with Tigger," I said. "She's just finishing her breakfast."

Cassie unsaddled her horse and led him into the pen while I held the gate open. She was smiling from ear to ear. "Let's go, Jas! Let's get started on that doghouse!"

I grinned back. "Mom and Dad are gone to town all day, but I still think we should work out of sight behind the barn." I led the way. "Then we can stow everything in the old shed if we don't finish today."

Cassie stood with her hands on her hips, surveying the place. A battered old toolshed leaned lopsided against the back of the barn, its doors lodged open by dirt and gravel. I went inside.

"I've got all the tools we'll need." I pulled them out of the box where I'd stashed them earlier that morning. "I was so excited I couldn't sleep," I admitted, "so I was out here at first light gathering things up."

On an old railroad tie, I lined up the hammer, a can of long nails, screwdriver, can of screws, a handsaw, and the metal measuring tape I'd gotten for my tenth birthday when I was obsessed with building birdhouses. "And, best of all, 'cause it's going to make the job super-easy. . . ." I held up Dad's electric circular saw and a long orange power cord.

"Good job, Jas." Cassie nodded at the tools. "We can build a mansion! If we just had some wood. . . ."

"Duh. I have that worked out, too."

I led the way to a crawlspace under the backside of the house, between the rosebushes. Moving aside a plywood panel, I squatted down and peered inside.

"I found this stuff last summer," I said. "Nobody will miss it." I stepped aside so Cassie could look into the dark space. "There are two-by-fours, one-by twos, everything we need to frame it up, and there's some plywood in the hayloft."

"Cool," she said. "I hope you don't think I'm going under there to haul that stuff out."

"No, I'll do it." I got down on all fours and ducked my head. "Should have brought a flashlight."

"Watch for snakes; rattlers love to hang out under houses. Nice and cool." Cassie grinned when she said it, pretending to help.

I started backing out. "Um . . . Maybe I better get a flashlight."

"You stay there. I'll get it," Cassie said and ran for the back door.

"Ay! Cuantos arañas!"I slapped a spider from my neck then started shuffling the two-by-fours, moving them toward the bright opening behind me. Where was Cassie with the flashlight? Something skittered in the dead leaves and debris farther under the house, back in the corner. I froze. It sounded bigger than a mouse.

"Here you go." All of a sudden she was shining the flashlight beam in my eyes.

I grabbed it and angled the light into the corner where I'd heard the rustling. Nothing. Pile of dry leaves. My heart was still thumping.

Cassie started pulling the boards out of the hole behind me as I handed them back. Eight two-by-fours, half a dozen planks. I laid down the flashlight and grabbed a heavy roll of tarpaper. "For the roof," I explained.

A gray mouse jumped out of the end of the tarpaper roll and ran across my hand.

"Ahh!" I dropped the tarpaper and backed out fast, falling over myself and into the rosebush. Cassie was on the ground, too, laughing and pointing at me.

"You should see your face!"

Now that I was safe outside, I could laugh at myself. "That's it," I said. "I'm not going back under there. No tarpaper."

"Well, one of us is going back."

"What for?"

"Flashlight." She pointed into the crawlspace where the yellow beam lit up a bit of the darkness.

"I'll get it." Cassie ducked into the darkness before I could say anything. She scrambled through the dirt and cobwebs, grabbed the flashlight, and popped back out. "Nothing scary under there!" she laughed.

I climbed up into the hayloft in the barn and retrieved two big sheets of plywood. I lay on my stomach to lower them down while Cassie reached up to grab them.

"All right, let's get to building," she said when we had all the wood and tools in front of us.

I felt a surge of gratitude toward my friend. Who else would help me get ready for a dog I didn't even have yet?

"I know a little bit about building," I said.

"I helped Pa build a chicken coop for Mrs. Riley last year," Cassie said, "so I think we can figure this out easy enough."

She started laying the wood out on the ground. "First, we frame it out with two-by-fours, then we use the plywood for the roof and walls and floor."

"It needs to be big enough for a medium-sized dog to stretch out in," I said, picturing my dog lying in his house, head on paws, looking out at me.

Cassie measured and marked the boards while I dragged one end of the extension cord around the corner of the barn and inside the door to the outlet.

We used the power saw to cut the plywood pieces and the handsaw for the two-by-fours. I was pretty sure I'd get in trouble for using Dad's power saw without asking, but plywood was just too hard to cut straight with a handsaw. I hoped that he'd be proud rather than mad when he saw the finished doghouse.

I held the uprights while Cassie nailed them in place. We used some planks for the floor. I didn't want my dog lying on the cold ground.

When the sides were framed in and the floor was nailed in place, we attached the plywood sides and finally, the roof.

"Let's hang the front over pretty far, so it shades the doorway," I said. Cassie and I looked at each other.

"Jeez! We forgot the door!" she laughed. "Very useful doghouse, with no way in!"

We spent another twenty minutes cutting a door and framing it out. "I'll hang a flap over it to keep the wind out later," I said. "And I'll put straw in it for bedding. But, you know he'll be sleeping with me mostly."

"I know. I have a feeling you two will be inseparable. Maybe we should have made the doghouse big enough for you *and* the dog."

"Ha-ha," I said. "Point is, he'll only stay out here when I'm at school or somewhere he can't come. A dog needs to be with his pack, his family, not tied up or fenced off somewhere alone."

We stood back and admired our work. The house was sturdy; a little lopsided, but it would do fine.

"Grab the other side. Mom and Dad will be home any minute."

We hauled the doghouse into the old toolshed. I hustled the saw and other tools back to Dad's workbench in the good toolshed by the house and hung the power cord on its nail in the barn. Then we kicked dirt over the fresh sawdust and stowed the lumber scraps between the shed and the barn.

"We did it." Cassie held her hand up for a high-five and I slapped it.

"I never could have made it so good and so fast by myself. Thanks, Cass."

"That's what friends do." She headed for the corral where Tig and Rowdy were leaning against each other, nose to tail, swatting flies off each other's faces. Cassie caught Rowdy and saddled him. I gave her a leg up and she settled into the saddle.

"See you on the bus tomorrow," she said, and started up the hill behind our house.

"Actually, you won't," I hollered after her. "Tomorrow's my first day of work! I'll be coming to school straight from the ranch."

"Then I'll see you at school, Working Man." She gave Rowdy a squeeze with her heels, let out a whoop, and they galloped up the hill.

My first day of work! I'd actually forgotten about it while we were so busy building the doghouse. So much was happening at once.

Chapter 11

The alarm on my bedside table buzzed and I knocked it off the pile of books. It got louder lying there on the floor. I opened my eyes and groped around for the glowing, buzzing clock. It blinked 5:00 A.M. I hit the button on top and sat up.

Five A.M. was as dark as midnight, as far as I could see out my bedroom window. The smell of coffee drifted in; I'd promised Dad I'd make it, but he had beaten me to it. I hoped I'd do better the rest of the day.

I pulled on my clothes and used the bathroom. In the mirror, I saw the tag from my T-shirt hanging under my chin. I pulled off the shirt and put it on frontwards. I double-checked: pants zipped, hair combed, boots on the right feet. Ready.

Before I even thought about breakfast, I went out to the barn and dug a scoop of feed out of the bin for Tig, threw her a flake of hay, and made sure her water trough was full.

Then I came back in and made bacon and scrambled eggs for Dad and me. I sat churning my eggs around on my plate.

"Better eat that, son," Dad said. "You'll starve, pushing those wheel lines around with nothing to burn in your stomach."

"Yeah," I replied, "just excited." I added, "And nervous."

Dad smiled. "You'll do fine. Just work hard and mind the boss."

"Yes, sir, I sure plan to." I hoped he was right that I'd do fine, that I'd keep up with the bigger guys and not make a fool of myself somehow.

I packed my lunch into my backpack with my books, since I'd be going straight from work to school.

Dad let me start the rig and sat beside me as I drove. The headlights lit the sagebrush lining the driveway. The yellow eyes of jackrabbits glowed beside the road then disappeared. I stopped where the gravel hit the paved road and we switched places. Dad drove us the rest of the way, pulling into the driveway at the Flying M just before six.

"You can let me out here." I didn't want anyone to see my dad dropping me off because I wasn't old enough to drive myself.

I guess he understood, because he stopped there at the end of the drive long enough for me to hop out and grab my bag. I watched him back out onto the road and head home. I waved. He stuck an arm out the window.

I walked the rest of the way up the drive toward the house. Three other guys stood shuffling their feet in the darkness in front of McPheeter's house.

I recognized one of the guys from school, a junior or

senior, I think. No friend of Colton's that I knew of, luckily.

He looked at me and grinned. "What do you think you're doing here, little man?"

"Same as you. Working," I said, pretending to size up the field next to the house, just sprouting with new hay.

"Well, all right, then," he said. He stuck out his hand. "They call me Tank. I've seen you around school."

"Oh yeah," I said, "you're on the football team, right?"

We talked for a few minutes, just like working men waiting to start our day. I was feeling bigger all the time.

A tall guy came out of the house, not Mr. McPheeter, but he looked a lot like him, just younger.

"I'm Dale," he said. "I'll be taking you out to the fields. Any problems or questions, you ask me."

"Hop on back," he told us and climbed into the cab of the flatbed truck. "Smiley, load up, boy." A little spotty cattle dog squirmed out from under the porch steps and leaped onto the truck bed.

We all piled on. It was a short, bumpy ride through the early morning light, maybe half a mile. We hopped off when the truck stopped at the open gate to a hay field between the road and the creek.

McPheeter's son gave us directions to space ourselves out along the line, one person to a wheel. When he said "Go!" I put both hands against the wheel and pushed. The wheel didn't budge; in fact, the pipe was bending on either side as the guys down the line rolled their wheels forward.

It was all going wrong first thing! Maybe I wasn't strong enough after all.

"Hey, kid!" Tank yelled from the next wheel down. "Use your shoulder, like this, until it gets unstuck."

I dug my feet in, trying to keep the weight on my good leg, and pushed with my shoulder. Sure enough, the wheel unstuck itself from the dirt and rolled slowly forward. Once it got going, it moved along more easily.

We rolled the length of sprinkler pipe forward a few yards across the fields. I wasn't real sure what I was doing, but Tank showed me how to tighten the joints and unclog the sprinkler heads as we went.

"Watch your head!" Tank yelled when a pipe came swinging fast toward me. I ducked.

"Hey, thanks," I said, breathless. It seemed like I'd made a friend.

We moved down the field to the next length of pipe, rolled it forward, tightened joints, and moved on. The low morning sun streamed down on us. I was sweating, even though the air was still cool.

We kept working for a solid two hours. Tank and I rolled the last wheel line into place. I looked down at my filthy shirt and jeans, smeared with mud and grass stains. "Guess it'd be smart to bring clean clothes next time." Tank and I both laughed at how we were going to look walking into school like this.

"Want a ride?" he asked me. "My truck's back at the ranch house."

"Sure." I grinned. We rode the flatbed back to the house, then climbed into Tank's white Chevy. I was sweaty and tired and starting to ache, but I felt good inside.

I was so excited the first day, I could hardly concentrate in class. Cassie caught up with me at lunch.

"So? How was the first day on the job? You're a mess!"

My boots were caked with mud and my jeans and shirt were splattered. I'd rinsed the dirt off my face and arms in the restroom, but still had chunks of mud in my hair. "Yeah, I already got called into the office for it. I'll bring clean clothes tomorrow."

"So, it was dirty," she said. "What else?" We climbed up on the low wall by the gym and sorted through our lunch bags while we talked.

"I did okay. Once I got started. It's hard, harder than I thought it would be." I could admit that to Cassie. "But I figured out I'll make a hundred and twenty dollars a week."

Cassie's eyes bugged out. "Wow! That's a lot of money! You'll have your dog in no time."

We talked some more and ate our lunches until the bell rang. Back to class. She was right. I'd have my dog in no time. Then it would be worth all the tiredness and sore muscles in the world. I just hoped I'd be able to keep it up for six whole weeks!

Chapter 12

Instead of getting easier, though, it got harder and harder to get up in the morning as that first week went on. Five o'clock seemed to come earlier each morning, like I'd just put my head down on my pillow and the alarm was ringing in my ear. I tried to go to bed early, but I had chores and homework to do every night.

On Wednesday, I fell asleep in history, my head resting on my desk. It felt so good to close my eyes, until Mrs. Litner slammed a book on my desk. I got assigned an extra essay as punishment, but at least she didn't call Mom and Dad.

At breakfast on Friday, Dad must have noticed me nodding off over my oatmeal.

"You all right, son? Is your leg giving you trouble?" he asked.

"No more than the other one," I said. "I'm just a little tired."

"Are you keeping up at school? Because if this job is too much, you'll have to let it go, at least until school's out."

"No! No, it's fine. I just have to get used to it. I promise. I'm keeping up."

"Well, we'll see."

"Please, Dad, this means everything to me." I hated to beg, but I had to make money now to get my dog, to get him trained by fair time. . . .

I could hardly keep my eyes open in class that Friday afternoon. When I tried to read along in social studies, the words wiggled and ran together on the page. I kept telling myself that it was just one more day until payday and on Sunday, I could sleep in.

After work on Saturday, when we'd all ridden the flatbed back to the ranch house, I lined up with the rest of the men to collect my wages.

Mr. McPheeter sat at a table on the porch and handed the money to each guy in line, making a note by his name in a tablet.

I held my head up high, trying not to grin too big. I ran my hat around and around in my hands. I'd done it; made it through a week of hard work. A spark of pride ran through me like tapping an electric fence wire.

When I stood in front of him, Mr. McPheeter looked up. "I heard you did a good job this week, Jasper."

"I did my best, sir."

"Keep it up," he said and handed me some bills. He looked down at his notebook and I turned to go.

"Jasper," he said.

My heart thumped; maybe it was a joke and I hadn't done well, and he was going to take back the money. . . .

"Always count your money while you're still in front of

the guy who gave it to you," he said. "That way, if there's a problem, it's plain to everybody."

"Yes, sir." I counted it out, five twenties and two tens, more money than I'd ever earned before. "All here. Thank you, sir."

Tank got his money and drove me to the bottom of my driveway. "I can pick you up on Monday, save your dad the drive," he said as I got out.

"Yeah, sure, that'd be great." I grinned. "I'll be down here at quarter till, that okay?"

"See ya then." Tank rattled off down the road.

Wow! Dad wouldn't have to give me a ride anymore. And I had all this money. I had my doghouse built. I'd have my dog before long. I'd beat Colton at the fair. I was on top of the world! I ran up the driveway, the week's tiredness falling away, at least for the moment.

I put all those tens and twenties into my "Dog Fund" cigar box. I aimed to bring it all out at dinner one night and show my folks how much I'd saved to buy dog food and get him his shots and maybe buy him a bed and some toys, if he was a toy-playing sort of dog.

But things can turn on a dime; I almost blew it that night. I nearly lost my job *and* my chance at getting the dog.

The excitement and all the early mornings caught up with me; I was dead tired by dinnertime. I picked at my food, got excused early, and went out to feed Tig.

"Hey, girl," I scratched her ears as she leaned over the fence, looking for her dinner.

I filled her feed pan with grain and threw a flake of hay in the manger. I did the dishes. Then I went in to bed.

A horrible screeching and squawking jerked me awake. Something was after the chickens! Had I closed up the coop last night? I couldn't remember. . . . I'd been so tired. I shook my head to clear it.

A skunk or raccoon could get into the pen easily enough; it was my job to close the chickens up safely in their wooden coop at night.

I pulled on my jeans and ran barefoot down the stairs, slammed out the back door, then back in to grab the flashlight.

Disaster!

I could see the coop doors gaping wide open. Feathers everywhere. A big gray shape lumbered down the ramp from the coop into the pen, a white chicken flailing and flapping in its mouth. A raccoon. It squinted into the flashlight beam then turned and scurried for the gaping hole it had torn in the pen wire.

I had to stop him or I'd never get my dog!

Chapter 13

"Hey!" I screamed, running toward the pen. "Drop that chicken!" Like he was going to listen to me. The chicken kicked and squawked and struggled to get away while the raccoon tried to push it through the hole in the wire.

I beat on the wire pen with the flashlight and yelled some nonsense. The raccoon dropped the chicken, squeezed through the hole, and headed for the brush by the creek. The chicken flapped and cackled around the pen.

"What happened?" Dad came panting out of the dark.

"Raccoon in with the chickens; I scared him off."

I went through the pen door and laid the flashlight on the ground. I cornered the scared chicken and picked her up. She had some blood on her neck, but struggled to get loose, so I guess she wasn't too hurt.

"I think she's okay," I said, not looking Dad in the eye. I knew what was coming.

"You forgot to close the coop up, didn't you?"

I didn't want to answer, but I had to. "Yeah, I guess so."

I let the chicken loose in the doorway of the coop and

she scampered in and flapped up with her sisters on their perches inside. I shut the door between the coop and the pen. I latched it and pulled it to be sure it was locked up tight. My heart felt like a lump in my chest, barely beating, rock heavy. "I'm so sorry, Dad, it won't happen again."

"No, it won't." Dad's voice was hard and tight. "That job is too much for you. We said you could keep it only if your chores and schoolwork didn't suffer."

"I know, but please, please. I'll do better. I'll do better, I promise. I'll never forget the chickens again. Oh, please, Dad." I couldn't stand the thought of losing my job, of losing my dog; I was getting so close.

Dad stood there looking at me for the longest minute ever. "We'll talk about it in the morning," he finally said.

As if I'd sleep any more that night.

I lay there for a long time wondering how I'd ever live without a dog. I guess I drifted off because I woke to the smell of coffee and the sound of voices downstairs.

I'm not usually the type to spy, but this was too important. I stationed myself at the top of the stairs, out of sight. I could hear Mom and Dad in the kitchen.

"It's *one* mistake. He's been working so hard." Wow, Mom was standing up for me.

A chair scraped, footsteps, coffee pouring. "More?" Dad asked.

"Just a half." Coffee pouring.

"I told him he had to keep up his chores and schoolwork," Dad said, "If we don't follow up on the rules we lay down. . . ."

"I know. I know. But he's been more responsible than any other kid his age, I bet. He wants that dog so much." She got that right, I thought.

I held my breath.

There was a long silence. Then he said it: "All right. One more chance."

I tiptoed back to my room, let out a huge whoosh of breath. What a relief! Everything was going to be okay. I dressed and went downstairs.

"Morning." I looked at the floor, like I thought I was in big trouble. I poured myself a glass of milk and sat down at the table. I looked from one of them to the other.

"Jasper," Mom started, "we appreciate how hard you've been working. Forgetting the chickens was a mistake, but we didn't lose any, so it could have been worse."

Dad rubbed his forehead and cleared his throat. "You can keep your job, but you need to promise you'll tell us if it gets to be too much, and no more forgetting chores, understood?"

I let loose a huge breath and nodded. "Thank you! You won't be sorry."

I never forgot to lock up the chickens again, you can bet on that. Coming that close to losing it all had fired me up. I stayed awake in school. I did all my chores.

During the next five weeks, I got used to getting up

early. I really liked the ride to work, waiting at the end of the driveway in the dark, climbing in beside Tank, listening to the radio on our way. I felt so grown up.

And I collected five more weeks of pay. I felt rich! I had more than enough money to buy my dog and take care of him.

When I got home from the last day of work, my pay in my pocket, I felt bigger and stronger than ever. I was ready.

While Dad dished up pieces of cherry pie, I brought down my Dog Fund cigar box.

I opened the box. "I have over six hundred dollars," I said, proudly.

"And that's not all." I showed them the collar and leash and then I led them outside. Out behind the barn I opened the doors to the old toolshed and showed them the doghouse. "Cassie and I built it."

"Oh, Jasper," Mom said, looking at me like I was a new person.

Dad looked the house over, bent down, and peered inside. "You two did a good job, son." He looked at Mom. She nodded.

"All right, Jasper; you've earned your dog," he said.

I never heard sweeter words! I jumped up and down and high-fived Dad. Then I grabbed Mom's hand and swung her around and around like we were at a barn dance.

"Thank you! Thank you! Wait 'til I tell Cassie!" I hollered.

Chapter 14

When I calmed down enough to hold still, we sat in the kitchen. Mom and Dad had another cup of coffee. I had another slice of Dad's cherry pie.

"Dad, you bake the best pie ever!" I said with my mouth full of sweet-sour cherries. "When can I get my dog? Tomorrow?"

"How about the first Saturday after school gets out? That's only two weeks away," Mom said.

Two whole weeks. Seemed like forever, but I guess I'd made it this long. . . .

"One thing, though," Mom sounded serious. "I want you to pick out a dog at the shelter, not from the paper or the neighbors."

"Okay." I didn't care where I got my dog. "But why?"

"The dogs at the shelter really need homes," she said. "They've been abandoned or abused or neglected." She looked me in the eyes to make sure I was getting the point.

"No problem, Mom! I'd love to save a dog." I was already there in my mind, lifting my pup out of the pen. . . .

I shoved the last forkful of pie into my mouth and

headed for the door to go tell Cassie the news. "Oh yeah, can I go to Cassie's?"

I heard Dad say, "Yep. Go on," when I was out the door and halfway to the back fence.

Instead of taking the time to saddle Tigger, I just ran. In fact, I felt guilty that I didn't even stop to tell my horse the news, but I figured Cassie should be the first to know. She'd stood by me and helped me all this time.

"Cassie? Hey, Cass!" I poked my head into the barn, leaning on the big swinging doors that stood propped open. The afternoon light streamed in the window of Rowdy's stall. The horse shook his head at me and pushed against the front of his stall. "Hey, boy, where's Cassie?"

Cassie popped up beside him with a hoof pick in her hand.

I jumped and she laughed. "What are you hollering about?"

"Guess what," I panted, out of breath from running. I blurted out the rest before she could open her mouth: "I'm getting my dog!"

"No way!" Cassie and I were both jumping up and down now. "Finally! Where? When? What kind?"

Rowdy caught our excitement, startled and stepped back, tossing his head. Cassie held his halter and stroked his nose to soothe him.

"At the shelter, first Saturday when school's out. Don't know what kind yet, but it'll be the best dog in the world."

"Of course," Cassie agreed. "Couldn't be anything else."

Cassie took a lead rope off the hook by the stall and clipped it to Rowdy's halter.

I followed as she led Rowdy out and turned him loose in the corral.

"It's two weeks until school's out, until I get him," I picked a stem of grass and chewed it while I thought. "What in the world am I going to do until then? How am I going to wait that long?"

Cassie turned on the hose and ran water into Rowdy's trough. "How about if we get ready to train him for the agility trials? Make an obstacle course. We can start him right away, well, as soon as he's settled in."

"That's perfect! We can make jumps and a tunnel and in-and-out poles." I could see it now; introducing my dog to each obstacle, taking him through it over and over until he got the knack. Then running beside him as he got faster and faster, faster than Colton and Fencer would ever be.

"Hey," Cassie snapped me out of my daydream. "Isn't that Colton's truck?"

Sure enough, I could just see the white truck crawling by out on the dirt road, Colton at the wheel.

"And there's Fencer." Cassie pointed. "He looks dead tired!" The black-and-white border collie ran just behind the truck, eating the dust spun up by the tires. The dog was panting hard, trying to keep up.

"He's roadworking him," I said. "I'd never train my dog that way. Lazy bum should get out and run with him."

Cassie nodded. "We'll do it the right way. And we'll win. You'll see."

Colton's ways were mean, but his dog was fast. . . . I hoped Cassie was right.

We spent all our spare time in the next two weeks building our practice course for training my dog. We did a little bit every afternoon we could get free for an hour or so, between chores and homework and meals.

In the flat field behind my barn, we raked away the horse manure and threw the biggest rocks in a pile. We rolled an old culvert pipe into the field for a tunnel. It was about three feet high and maybe eight feet long.

Our jumps were made of old fence poles. And an upside-down water tub was our "pause" stand, where the dog would sit still until called. We pounded six metal t-posts, the kind that hold up barbwire fencing, about three feet apart in a row for weave poles. The dog would weave in and out between them at a run.

Finally, an old plank on a log made the seesaw for the dog to walk up one side, tip it, and go down the other. And a tire swing hung between two posts a couple feet off the ground was our jump-through.

Two weeks later, we looked over our course. Three jumps, in-and-out poles, tire jump, tunnel, and seesaw. It was a long way from being the real thing, but it would do to teach the commands and how to follow my lead from one obstacle to the next.

"And there's one more thing," Cassie said. "We're

gonna need a plank wall that Willie has to climb up and over."

I looked around and found two old wooden doors behind the toolshed. We dug holes on either side and planted sturdy posts, then nailed the doors sideways against the posts, one door atop the other, flat sides making a wall almost as tall as me.

"Looks good," I said and high-fived Cassie.

Cassie lay back in the short grass beside me. "Now all you need is the *right* dog."

"Tomorrow!" I grinned at her. "Tomorrow I'll be bringing that dog home."

Chapter 15

I'll remember it forever; the day I met my dog.

As Mom and I got out of the car in the animal shelter parking lot, a riot of barking started up.

Dogs in the outside kennels along the side of the building jumped against their chain-link gates. Baying hounds, yipping little dogs, sharp-barking mutts. Dozens of dogs, all trying to get our attention. How would I choose? I could only take home *one* dog!

Mom led me through a metal door that read "ADOPTIONS."

It was a little quieter inside. An older lady behind a metal desk looked up and smiled at us. "Hi, how can I help you?"

A fluffy white cat with one eye and a torn-off ear sat on the corner of the desk, licking her paw. I stroked the cat's head. Mom nudged me with her elbow.

"I'm here to pick out a dog," I told the woman.

She smiled and pointed. "Right through those doors. Jill is working back there if you see one you want to meet."

"Thanks."

Mom followed me through the heavy metal doors.

The barking got louder the minute we walked in. Much louder. It echoed all around us, bouncing off the concrete walls. I felt like covering my ears, but I didn't want Mom to think I couldn't handle a few dogs barking.

Chain-link kennels lined the hallway. Each kennel held at least one dog, some of them had two or even three. There must have been a hundred dogs here. How was I going to know which one was for me? What if I picked the wrong one?

The barking was already driving me crazy. In the first kennel on one side, a big kinky-haired tan and black dog bounced straight up about five feet high. Every time he came down, he barked louder than the bounce before. He landed with a paw in his empty food bowl and sent it clattering against the wall.

I moved on down the line. In the next cage, a little white terrier yipped and ran in circles, barking the whole time. Fast and agile, for sure, but way too yappy for me!

"Seems like everyone wants our attention," Mom said. She was smiling grimly, like she wanted to cover her ears, too. She wandered on down the hallway, peering into each kennel, setting off even louder barking down the line.

Kennel after kennel. I looked in each one. There were big dogs and little dogs, hounds and shepherds and fluffy little lap dogs, all of them barking and barking, throwing themselves against the wire or jumping up in the air. My head got all muddled with the noise and commotion. None of them seemed right; I couldn't picture any of them lying at the foot of my bed. . . .

Only one big white dog lay on its blanket, looking the other way. Not barking, just lying there. I put my fingers through the wire, "Hey, boy," I said. Quick as a flash, the dog snarled, leapt up, and hurled itself at the cage door. I let out a yelp and jumped back. It actually bit at the chain-link door trying to get at me. Then I saw the sign on the kennel door: "DO NOT TOUCH! DOG UNDER OBSERVATION."

I was shaking from the surprise and from how fierce he was. That wasn't the dog for me, for sure. Maybe I wouldn't find the right dog here after all. Maybe all my excitement and hope was for nothing.

I jumped at a voice behind me. I hadn't heard anyone coming over all the noise.

"Sorry about that dog," a young woman in a green smock and jeans said loudly over the barking hubbub. She motioned toward the white dog who was lying on his blanket again, his head on his paws. "He came in as a stray yesterday and is still really scared and shook up. Poor guy."

"We came for a puppy," Mom told her.

"I'm Jill." She held out her hand to Mom first, then to me, and we both shook it. She leaned toward me. "I'm sure you'll take really good care of a puppy and have a lot of fun together."

"The puppies are all down here," she said over her shoulder. Mom and I followed her down the hallway.

She stopped in front of a pen full of little wriggly

brown and black puppies. "Now these are a shepherd mix," Jill said, opening the gate. She picked up the closest pup. The other pups all whined and jumped and clambered over each other, a furry, squealing pile.

"Oh, they're adorable!" Mom laughed and held her hand up to her mouth. Her eyes softened. "Look, Jasper! Aren't they cute?"

Jill scratched the little brown pup under the chin while the dog's pink tongue shot out, licking her nose. "They'll be medium-sized dogs, really smart. Good watchdogs and companions."

I moved closer and petted the puppy Jill held. It whimpered and nibbled my fingers with its sharp baby teeth. Its fur was soft as velvet and its little tongue was warm and smooth.

The clamor of the barking dogs excited the puppy even more and it squirmed and yipped in Jill's arms.

"These pups will be adopted quickly, so if you want one, you should take it today," Jill said.

"Which one do you want, Jasper?" Mom asked.

Something in me hesitated. I only got to choose once; I wanted to make absolutely certain I got the right dog.

"Um, they're really cute," I looked off down the long hallway of kennels, the desperate, barking dogs, homeless, unloved. What would happen if no one chose them? "I'm going to look a little more."

I left Mom and Jill with the puppies. "Jasper," Mom said as I walked off, "just choose a puppy and let's go."

I think the barking was getting to her, too. She sounded tired and impatient.

I kept going. More dogs. Big dogs, little dogs, beagles and pit bulls and Labs. I had to choose, but I couldn't. My head hurt; too many choices, the barking bouncing off the walls, Mom trying to hurry me.

Then I saw him. The big, shaggy black dog sat calmly in his kennel, looking up at me. He didn't bark. He didn't jump. He didn't dance around or hurl himself at the wire. He just sat there looking at me.

He must have weighed a hundred pounds, a big, solid dog. He cocked his head at me and I could see that his eyes were strange, milky blue instead of brown or green, like most dogs. His eyebrows stood up like dry bunchgrass and he had a droopy black moustache. His mouth was opened a little, like he was smiling. He looked like a kindly, wise old man.

My heart leaped in my chest. His tail wagged slowly, sweeping the concrete floor. He liked me, too!

The crazy barking and yelping and baying faded out as I stared at him. The kennel stink of pee and cleaners disappeared.

I felt something moving between the dog and me, him and me in our own silence. I couldn't take my eyes off him.

Chapter 16

Mom! Look at him." I knelt on the cold concrete and strung my fingers through the chain-link kennel door. Mom came up beside me and stood in front of the kennel, her arms crossed over her chest.

"Oh, honey. Come back and pick a puppy."

The big dog got up slowly and took a step toward me, his feathery tail wagging. He stood with his nose a few inches from my face, sniffing and sniffing through the wire. Mom stood behind me with her hands on her hips. I could feel her frown like it was dripping down the back of my neck.

Without looking up, I said, "I can't explain it, Mom. It's like he's telling me he belongs with me. I think he's the one." I could picture this big black dog lying on the foot of my bed as clear as day. I could see him following along as I rode Tigger over the hills.

Mom read the yellow plastic-covered card hanging from the kennel door.

"Jasper," she put her hand gently on my shoulder. "That dog is old and blind. He can't even see you."

I looked into his milky blue eyes. Blind? Really? I was sure he was looking at me.

Mom went on, "He's got cataracts, like Grandma got, remember? His owners gave him up because he's hard to care for. A blind dog? How would he get around? How could he play with you?"

Mom knelt beside me. "A dog like this won't be around much longer, but a puppy will be your friend for years and years."

I stood up and read the kennel card myself. "Intake Date: January 10th. Owner Surrender. Pet Name: Willie. Senior. Giant Schnauzer Mix. Extra-Large. Male. Neutered. Fee: $30."

"But, Mom, he's been here for months!" I hated to think of him in this cold cage with nothing but a ratty blanket all this time. "And he's already been neutered and he's cheaper than the others."

I walked a little way down the hall, reading the price off the other cards. The dogs raised even more of a ruckus as I moved along and I practically had to shout. "Fifty. Fifty. Seventy-five. Look, this Dalmatian is a hundred bucks!"

As I walked back to Willie's kennel, I wondered: how am I going to convince my mom how important this dog is to me? How I could already tell we belonged together? That there was no way I could leave him here in this noisy place, inside that concrete and wire pen. My heart hurt just thinking about leaving him behind.

I would just have to take a stand and not budge, as my

grandpa would say, "Come heck or high water."

A look passed between Mom and Jill, a look that said, Kids! What do they know?

"Can I take him out?" I asked.

"Sure, if it's okay with Mom," Jill looked over for Mom's approval.

"A puppy would be better, Jasper."

"But, Mom," I tried not to whine. "You said the whole thing about getting a dog from the shelter was to save them, that they need good homes. Well, who's going to save Willie? Who's going to come for him? No one but me."

When she didn't say anything, I went on, "Willie needs me more than any other dog in here. And I need him."

"All right," Mom sighed. "You can walk him."

Jill opened Willie's gate and stepped inside the enclosure. My heart beat faster. She clipped the leash onto his collar. Willie stood beside her, his big feet planted wide. "Remember, he can't see you," Jill said. "Talk to him before you touch him, so he knows you're there."

"Hi, Willie. I'm Jasper." He looked up toward my voice and wagged his tail. I knelt down and held my hand under his nose while he got a good sniff, then I gently scratched his chin. Willie licked my face. His tongue was so big! I laughed and wiped my face with my sleeve.

Jill handed me his leash. I coiled it up short in my hand, so Willie walked close to my side. We followed Jill down the corridor of barking dogs. Willie leaned away from the noise, warm against my leg.

We broke out the end door into the fresh air and went through a gate into a big pen. Willie tossed his head and his tongue lolled out. I swear he was smiling at being out in the sun, out of the noise. Maybe he felt as hopeful of a new beginning as I did.

"Usually, we let the dogs run around off-lead in here," Jill said, shutting the gate behind her. "But you might want to walk him around on the leash, so he doesn't run into the fence."

Jill turned to Mom. "A blind dog can learn the perimeters of his yard pretty easily, but he hasn't been out here much. When he's in an unfamiliar place, he's safest on a leash."

I thought I'd be leading Willie around, so I talked to him, telling him it was okay, that he was safe with me. Turns out, Willie walked me like I was the blind one.

He strode out with his big black nose to the ground, smelling the dozens of dogs that had been in the pen before him. He crossed the grass like he could see just fine and I gave his leash a little tug when he got near the fence on the other side. He turned, just like that, and sniffed along the base of it to the next corner. Willie peed on just about every post and bush in that yard. Every other dog would know that he'd been there.

Jill and Mom were watching us. Mom had a sour, sad look on her face. Jill was saying "When an animal, or a person, for that matter, loses one sense, the others get stronger. He can probably hear and smell better than most dogs here."

We circled past them and trotted to the far end of the pen. It was like no one else existed but Willie and me. Me and my dog.

At the other end, Willie turned and bounded, actually took three big leaps across the grass, like he knew how far it was and that there was nothing in his way until then. I laughed and ran to keep up, the leash still in my hand. He skidded to a stop a couple feet from the fence. He looked at me with his blind blue eyes and smiled a big wide grin.

I hugged him and rubbed my face in the thick fur of his neck. I whispered, "You're mine, Willie. Mine."

I looked up at Mom. "Please," I said quietly. "Please, Mom."

She turned to Jill, "If there are problems, can we bring him back?"

"Of course. But I think we'd have to keep Jasper here, too." Jill smiled at me. "I don't think you're ever going to get them apart."

She was right.

I guess Mom saw how determined I was, because she gave in. We signed the adoption papers; I handed the lady in the office my money, and we took Willie home.

Chapter 17

I've never had a happier ride home from anywhere. I rode in the backseat with Willie, my arm around his neck.

After a few miles, he lay down on the seat with his big heavy head on my leg and shut his eyes. I rubbed his stomach in slow circles and stroked his soft ears.

I caught Mom's eye in the rearview mirror as we started down our road. The tired little lines around her eyes disappeared for a minute. "You sure look happy," she said. And she was right.

"Come on, boy." I got out and gave his leash a tug. "I want you to meet my horse, Tig. The three of us are going to spend a lot of time together."

"Aren't you going to bring him in for your dad to see?" Mom asked.

I guess I was nervous about showing him to Dad. He might not like Willie. What if he just wouldn't let me have a blind dog? Would he make me take him back?

"Yeah," I replied. "I think he has to pee first and I want him to meet Tigger. We'll be there in a sec."

Willie strutted out into the tall-grassed orchard, just like he could see. He stopped to pee on every other clump of rye. He was so confident!

I took him into the barn all hung with afternoon shadow. How much could he see? Light and dark? Only blackness? He sneezed in the dusty barn and sniffed his way from empty stall to stall. Jill was right; his sense of smell led him around, just like he could see.

At the pasture fence, I called my horse over. "Tigger, come meet Willie." Tig trotted across the paddock with her head down and her neck stretched out. I doubt the horse had ever seen a dog so big and black and hairy.

"Willie, this is Tigger. You two and Cassie are my best friends now, so you all have to get along."

No sooner were the words out of my mouth then Willie bolted under the fence, yanking the leash from my hand. He must have smelled something irresistible, like fresh horse poop, because he took off with his nose to the ground. Tig backed off fast, facing the big dog who was sauntering across her corral.

"Willie!" I slid through the fence slats. Tig danced closer and snorted. If Tig saw Willie as a threat, like a wolf or coyote, she'd try to trample him.

Sure enough, Tigger turned and trotted toward Willie, her ears laid back and nostrils flaring. She reared up and boxed the air with her front hooves. I ran between Willie and Tigger.

"No, Tig! Get back!" I hollered. I flung my arms out,

waving the horse off. She came thudding down, one hoof catching my shoulder. I yelped as I fell. Willie stiffened up and growled.

Tig tossed her head and trotted to the far side of the corral and faced us again. Would she charge at Willie now that I was in the corral too?

Willie whined and came right to me where I sat in the dust. "Good boy." I rubbed his ears. "I'm okay," I reassured him, trying to keep the tremble out of my voice. The horse trotted toward us, ears still pinned back.

I stood up a little shaky. "Get away, Tig!" I shouted and waved my arms again. The horse stood her ground, her eyes never leaving Willie, but came no closer.

I rubbed my shoulder. Luckily, Mom had already gone into the house. The last thing I needed was an "I told you so."

I grabbed the leash and led Willie out of the corral, keeping one eye on my horse. Tig trotted a few feet closer and flared her big nostrils and tossed her head.

"Oh, get over it," I told her, feeling braver, now that we were out of reach.

Willie went on sniffing his way down the fence line, like he hadn't just about gotten trampled by a thousand-pound animal. I was still shaken up from Tig's charging at Willie. What if they never learned to get along?

I walked Willie back into the barn, out of sight of the house. I rolled up my sleeve to see where Tig had hit me with her hoof. It was red and sore, but not turning black and blue, so I guess nothing was broken. I was lucky. I'd known plenty of people who'd had bones broken by horses; falling off, getting kicked and stepped on.

When we finally went in the kitchen door, Mom and Dad were drinking coffee at the wooden table, a plate of cookies between them. Dad liked to do a bit of baking. The cookies smelled sweet and chocolaty and I grabbed two to calm my nerves. Willie sat down beside me.

"So that's him?" Dad said. Clearly, Mom had warned him that I hadn't fallen for a puppy after all. "What is he? Breed-wise, I mean."

"He's a giant schnauzer mix," I said proudly.

"But he's blind," Dad said, "and old. Is that right? Come here, big guy." He held his hand out and Willie cocked his ears toward Dad, stood up, and sniffed his hand.

I was on one knee now, rubbing and scratching Willie's big head. "I can't really explain it, Dad, just that I knew he was the one for me."

He and Mom sighed at each other and it rose like a cloud between them. Yep, it was going to take some time for everyone to get used to each other. That's okay, I thought. I've got time.

"You'll see. He'll get along fine." But after the trouble with Willie and Tigger, even I wasn't so sure.

Chapter 18

The big day had worn us both out. I left Willie snoring in the living room, next to Dad's chair, while I did my chores. Dad absentmindedly rubbed Willie's ears while he read a magazine. They were getting along!

I fed Tig and gave her a talking to about being nice to Willie, then I locked the chicken house up tight, to keep out the skunks and raccoons.

When I came back in, I woke Willie up and clipped the leash to his collar. I'd have to lead him around in the house until he learned where everything was. "Night, Mom, night, Dad." I led my tired dog toward the stairs.

"Night, Jasper," they said together.

I held Willie's collar and tapped each stair riser with my toe and said, "Step up, step up." He lifted each paw in a high-step and up the stairs we went, slow but sure.

I patted my bed and tugged the leash. Willie climbed up onto my bed. He stretched out across the foot of the bed, I mean, all the way across, because he was a *big* dog. I put on my pajamas and crawled under the covers.

I woke up a couple times during the night. Willie had

snuggled up next to me until he was lying right up against my side. His big body felt so warm against me. I rubbed his stomach a little and gently pulled his ears through my fingers and drifted back into sleep.

The sun streamed through my bedroom window when I heard a soft whine in my ear. It took me a minute to think what the sound could be.

"Oh, Willie," I rolled over to face him. "Good morning! Do you need to go outside, boy?" Our first full day together. I grinned at the thought of it. "Come on, Dad makes pancakes on Sundays."

I pulled on my jeans and headed downstairs. He followed the sound of my footsteps, and probably my smell, which was pretty strong, since I hadn't taken a bath last night.

I took the first five or six steps down the stairs before Willie crashed into me from behind. He couldn't see that the floor had ended and I was starting down the stairs. His feet went out from under him and he bump-bumped down on his belly. His chin hit a step with a horrible crack.

What had I done! "Oh, Willie, are you okay?" I should have tapped the stairs with my foot. I should have held his collar and led him down slowly. I hefted him to his feet, but he had trouble standing on the stairway. He stood there dazed and kind of tilting in against the stairs.

I eased him down the rest of the steps, holding his body as best I could, in case he fell again.

Dad's voice came from the kitchen, "Everybody okay? What was that thump?"

How stupid of me! I felt hot tears well up in my eyes. "Yeah, we're fine," I said. "Just getting used to the stairs."

At the bottom of the stairs, I felt him all over. He didn't flinch or yelp, even when I stroked his chin. I gently pried his mouth open. No broken teeth.

"Lo siento. I'm so sorry, Willie. It'll never happen again," I told him. "I'll keep you safe now. I will." I hugged him around the neck.

"Well there he is!" Dad knelt down and gave Willie a good scratch when we came into the kitchen.

"Ten minutes to breakfast," I heard behind me as I grabbed his leash from the hook by the door and led Willie out.

He put his nose to the ground and retraced our way to the orchard from the night before. What a nose! He peed on the exact same clumps of grass again.

I took him over to Tigger's corral. The horse trotted in a big circle, watching us approach, then came to the fence.

"Sit, boy," I told Willie.

Tigger came close, snorted, and backed up. She stood eyeing us for a minute, then came up to the fence. She stretched her head sideways between the rails and drew in the dog's scent. Willie growled a little as she ran her nose over his fur, ruffling it with her breath.

"Hush, boy." I held his collar tight. "It's okay."

When Tig was satisfied she pulled her head back through.

The mare went back to nibbling the short grass at the

edge of the corral. Willie sniffed along the outside of the fence, following her along.

"That's what I'm talking about!" I smiled, looking from one of them to the other.

I fed Willie on the back porch, which was more of a mudroom with a door to the inside and one to the outside. He had no problem smelling out his food bowl. I splashed my fingers in his water bowl, and patted the folded blanket I'd laid down back there for him.

"You stay here and eat your breakfast, buddy." I liked the sound of him crunch, crunch, crunching. "I have to go apply myself to a big stack of pancakes, and then I'm going to call Cassie and tell her all about you."

That reminded me of our obstacle course and the agility trials. Colton and Fencer. Would a blind dog be able to compete? Could he make it through the course? What would happen to all our plans if he couldn't do it? But it would be so amazing if he could!

Chapter 19

I dialed Cassie's number as soon as it was a civilized hour to call, which, according to my mom is nine o'clock. "He's here!" I said.

"The puppy? What kind did you get? It's a boy, right? Wait, don't tell me, I'll come right over." She hung up before I could answer even one of her questions.

I was rinsing breakfast dishes when Cassie burst through the front door, calling out, "Hey, it's me."

She stopped, hands on her hips, and stared at Willie, who was sitting beside me at the sink.

"Cassie, this is Willie," I said.

"Wow! That's no puppy. He's huge!" Cassie gaped at him.

"He's a giant schnauzer mix."

She came closer and peered at his face. "What's the matter with his eyes?"

"He's got cataracts," I said. "He's blind."

Cassie looked at me like I had two heads.

"So, you picked an old blind dog?" She said it more like a fact than out of meanness.

"More like he picked me." I stroked Willie's head and he smiled up at me. "Once I saw him, I knew I couldn't leave the shelter without him. It's hard to explain."

She got down on her knees and put the back of her hand up to his nose to sniff.

"Hi, Willie, I'm Cassie." Willie licked her hand, and then made a swipe from her chin to her forehead.

"Well, I guess you and your dog won't be beating Colton and Fencer at the fair, eh?" Cassie said.

"You mean just 'cause he's blind?" I felt protective of my dog. "Or because he's old?"

"Both."

I thought about it. "But what if he could do it? Wouldn't that be even better than beating them with a regular dog? You know, a healthy, young dog who can see where he's going?"

Cassie was quiet for a minute. "I don't know, Jasper. It's not going to be easy, that's for sure. But I guess we won't know unless we try," she said. "Who knows, you could have the first blind agility dog!"

I knelt down and hugged my dog tight to my chest. "You hear that, Willie? We're going to beat Colton and Fencer and you're going to be a star!"

That part, I wasn't sure of, but I was ready to try. We had to try.

The next day, Cassie and I stood behind the barn, looking over our obstacle course.

"The best way is to introduce him to one thing

at a time." Cassie knew about training animals. She'd taught Rowdy to barrel race and helped her uncle train his sheepdogs.

She went on, "Lead him up to the tunnel, the culvert pipe, let him sniff it all over, then lead him through it."

"Come on, Willie." Our first obstacle. He sniffed the open end of the pipe then all down the length of it and around the other end. Then he lifted his leg and peed on it.

I laughed, "You can't do that on the course, Willie. It'll slow us down!"

I ducked and started crawling into the pipe pulling Willie behind me. "Come on, boy."

"Use the commands so he learns them," Cassie called out.

"Oh yeah, 'Through' boy, 'through!'" I tugged the leash. Willie put one foot into the pipe. His toenails clicked on the aluminum. The metal must have felt funny under his foot. He stepped back and planted his feet.

I tugged a little harder. "Come on, Willie, it's all right. Through, through!" Willie sat down.

"Great! Can't even get him past the first obstacle." I shook my head, dismayed.

"Keep trying." Cassie started toward the house. "I'll be right back."

I was still sitting inside the pipe and Willie was still sitting outside when Cassie came back a few minutes later.

"Try this." She handed me some hot dogs, broken in pieces. "Your dad gave them to me."

Willie stood up and wagged his tail, smelling the meat.

This time, when I tugged the leash, Willie barely hesitated before stepping into the tunnel.

"Give him a piece about halfway through," Cassie's voice echoed from one end of the tunnel. "And keep giving him the command."

Willie and I made our way slowly through the pipe, his nails going click-click-click all the way. We popped out the other end. I petted and patted and hugged Willie. "Good dog! You did it!"

"Good job, guys! Now, take him through it a few more times."

Willie and I got faster and faster at crawling through the culvert pipe. Finally, I said, "I'm out of hot dogs." I rubbed my knees. "And my knees hurt."

"That's enough for today," Cassie said. "Tomorrow, we'll teach him to go through the pipe on his own, then we'll introduce him to the jumps."

We were really training my dog for the trials! It wasn't exactly like I'd imagined, what with Willie being blind, but it was happening just the same. Now, if we could get fast enough, we really *could* beat Colton and Fencer.

The next day, Cassie held Willie at one end of the pipe while I called from the other end. Willie perked his ears up at my voice echoing through the metal pipe; he trotted right through to me!

"Good boy!" He was so brave, so confident. I felt a surge of pride and love for my dog.

Cassie lowered the hanging tire down until the bottom edge rested on the ground. Willie sniffed it and scrambled through when I pulled his leash from the other side.

"Even though he's just stepping through it, use the command, 'Jump!'" Cassie advised.

"Jump!" I said right when he stepped through. "Good boy!"

"Now," Cassie said, "we gradually raise it up so he has to step higher and then actually jump through."

We shortened the ropes that held the tire between the two posts until it hung a couple inches off the ground.

He did all right stepping through, but it took a few more hot dogs to get him off the ground. I ran a piece of hot dog under his nose and lured him through the raised tire. He didn't actually jump, but kind of climbed and clambered through.

"What if he never does jump?" I was feeling a little discouraged. "How can we beat Colton and Fencer?"

"First rules of animal training: patience, patience, and more patience," Cassie said. "You give up too easy. Let's skip the jumping for now. Try the in-and-out poles."

He did better at that. He could feel the metal posts and leaned against them as he wove in and out. I guess a blind dog has to devise ways to deal with the world, just like a blind person.

The days and weeks ticked by. After a month of training, Willie dashed right through the tunnel, climbed through the tire if it wasn't too high, dodged between the in-and-out poles like a pro, and trotted up and down the seesaw. But, he stumbled and blundered into the pole jumps. And the vertical wall? Just another pee stop to Willie. Once he put his two big front paws up on the wall, stood on his hind legs, and barked. That was the closest he got to scaling the wall.

Cassie and Willie and I sat in the shade of the chestnut tree in the corner of the field after our latest training session.

"If the course at the fair just has a low tire jump, an old culvert pipe, and some in-and-out poles, we're going to do fine," I said, scratching Willie behind the ears. "Otherwise, we'll never beat Colton and Fencer."

The fair was only a month away, but instead of looking forward to beating Colton and Fencer, I was worried that we wouldn't be able to compete at all. I loved my dog with all my heart, but could he do it? Could he even finish the course?

Chapter 20

Summer was hot and dry, with more wildfires flaring up across the grasslands. Thunderclouds reared up on the horizon most afternoons.

We watched the sky as we ran Willie through our obstacle course again and again. We trained between chores and meals and more chores.

Before we knew it, pickups hauling horse trailers lined the road to the fairgrounds. Only a few days left until we faced Colton and Fencer; I was nervous as heck.

The county fair and rodeo was the biggest event of the summer, bigger even than the Fourth of July fireworks. Cassie was signed up for the barrel races. I usually did roping, but this year, it was all about the agility trials. That was all I cared about.

At the fairgrounds, people wandered in and out of the stuffy, hot exhibit buildings all week. It was a chance for folks to show off their skills. Vases full of flowers wilted in the heat, homegrown carrots and lettuce slumped on their paper plates, waiting to be judged for their size and color and shape. The arts and crafts took the heat better; paintings, quilts, homespun wool, woodcrafts, and metalwork. Pies and cakes and cookies sweated in glass cases.

In the livestock barns, sheep and calves kicked up dust in their stalls, looking hot and bored. People petted goats and rabbits and looked at all sorts of birds: fancy red pheasants and speckled guinea hens and chickens of every color. Men and women in fancy Western gear rode between the arena and barns on horses with silver bridles and ribbons braided in their manes.

The 4-H kids' pigs and sheep and steers got auctioned off on Thursday. Friday was Family Night, with stick-horse races for the littlest kids and "mutton-bustin'," which was like bull riding only with kids clinging to running, bucking sheep. The dog trials were Saturday afternoon, after the barrel racing and before the big rodeo. The fair ended with a live band and big street dance on Saturday night.

Saturday morning, I helped Cassie unload Rowdy from his trailer and saddle him up. She'd compete in the barrel races in a half hour. While they went to practice in the exercise pen, I wandered around between the horse trailers, letting Willie sniff all the strange-dog smells on the tires, trying to calm my nervous stomach and racing thoughts.

A deep and menacing voice, one I knew all too well, came from the other side of a big six-horse hauler. Willie growled low and fierce, like an old man muttering-mad. I laid a hand on his head, but he wouldn't be quieted.

Someone was crying, a quiet, scared sound. And Colton's voice, with its familiar knife-edge of threat: "Be quiet, you little whiner. I got business and you're gonna stay right here 'til I come for you."

A small girl's whimper said, "But I want to look at the horses. I don't want to sit here by myself all day."

"Yeah, well what you want don't matter. And don't you even think of telling Pa. When he asks, you say, 'We had a fine time at the fair.'"

"But . . ." she started.

SMACK! I heard a loud slap and a startled yelp. Willie jumped to his feet and growled louder. I stroked his head while he strained toward the noise.

I knew I should jump in to help, but fear held me like a coiled snake. I didn't move. I wish I had.

"You better be sitting right here when I come back for you."

Colton came around the corner so fast I barely had time to pull Willie behind the next trailer. Colton had his head down, though, and didn't see me.

Peeking out from behind the trailer, I saw Colton wave to Ketz, who was striding over from the gravel parking lot. Colton never looked back toward his little sister as he and Ketz climbed the slope toward the exhibition barns.

Willie led me to the dirty wreck of a trailer, the one that usually sat mired in the overgrown grass of Colton's yard. A girl about five or six years old sat on the running board. She wore a pink-flowered dress with shiny Sunday shoes and a little silver cross on a chain around her neck. A red handprint covered most of one cheek and tears cut through the dust on her face.

She startled upright when she saw us, and then dropped her head. I guess we didn't look any too dangerous. Willie walked right up and buried his nose in her hunched-over belly. She cradled his head and her tears soaked into his fur.

"You okay?" I squatted next to her. "I'm Jasper." She didn't say anything. "You're Colton's sister, right? What's your name?"

"Ginny," she sputtered, "Virginia."

"That's a pretty name. Can I sit down?" No response but a long, snotty inhale.

"You pulled the short straw when they gave out brothers," I said, sitting on the running board next to her. "I go to school with Colton. Believe me; I know how mean he can be."

I kind of stalled out. Comforting little girls wasn't my specialty. "I walk a little odd, 'cause I've got one short leg," I offered. "Your brother thinks it's hilarious."

Ginny looked up at me and wiped a sleeve across her nose. Both her hands kneaded the thick fur of Willie's neck. "One time," I said, "he twisted my arm so hard I thought it was busted. I could barely fork hay for a week."

"Yeah?" she said.

"Yeah." I fingered the loop on Willie's leash. "I just try to weather it and get on with things. You know, I think about all the good I've got, like my folks, and Willie here, and my horse, Tig."

"I might get a pony next year." She offered it like an attempt at getting on with life.

"That's great!" I said. "What kind you gonna get?" Willie continued comforting her, nuzzling the little girl's face and neck and blinking his milky blue eyes like a big flirt. Ginny and I talked a while more about horses, until she'd stopped crying altogether.

"You want to go watch the barrel races with us?" I stood up and stretched, trying to seem casual. Willie did his dog stretch beside me: front paws out, head down, butt in the air. Ginny smiled.

Then she shook her head, eyes on the ground again. "I best wait here," she whispered. Her tears started to brim up.

"All right." I didn't like leaving her, but I didn't want to miss seeing Cassie compete. I dusted my black hat on my leg. "It's going to be okay."

What a lame thing to say, I thought, as Willie and I walked away. But, really, what else could I do? She'd just have to sit there all day waiting for Colton to finish having his fun. Then he'd pick her up and they'd go on home. And he'd lie to his pa. Willie pulled back on his leash like he wanted to stay with Ginny.

The little girl wandered around in my mind as we walked to the arena. Maybe I should report Colton to the deputy?

But I didn't. If only I had.

Chapter 21

I sat in the bleachers with Willie and watched Cassie and Rowdy win the blue ribbon in the girl's barrel racing. I stood and cheered as she rode by, holding the ribbon high and beaming at me.

Only an hour until the agility trials. The setup crew moved the barrels out of the arena and hauled in the obstacles for the dogs. I crossed my fingers, praying that there wouldn't be a high wall or too many jumps.

Cassie came up and leaned against the rail.

"You and Rowdy did great," I said. I told her about Ginny. "Maybe we could go check on her after the trials."

"Yeah," she said, "and we should tell the deputy. Colton is a number one jerk."

The thought of telling on Colton made me nervous. If *he* got in trouble, well, next time I ran into him *I'd* be in trouble. He'd beat me up worse than he ever had, I was sure.

"We'll help Ginny after you and Willie win your race. She'll be okay sitting there for a little while more." Cassie tipped her hat back on her head. "So, are you ready?"

"I guess we better be." There was no backing out now.

"There they are." Cassie pointed across the arena.

Colton and Fencer were watching the setup from the other side. He saw us and smirked. I'm pretty sure Colton had no idea we were going up against him, probably thought he had it all sewn up, just like last year, and the year before. Even if the odds were against us, and they were, Willie and I would give him a run for his money.

Colton was a jerk and a bully. I thought of poor Ginny, sitting back there crying. I should have told on him.

"Ignore him. Let's go get your map and walk the course."

"Cass," I shook my head and smiled, "you're always so darn practical."

The cool thing about agility competitions is that any kind of dog could compete. There were different classes, according to size and the obstacles were geared for each class. Big dogs got big jumps, little dogs got small jumps. And the setup was always different, so the handlers got a map of the layout and got to walk the course ahead of time.

Cassie and Willie and I circled the arena to the judge's platform.

Colton and Fencer were already walking the course. He stopped and watched us. I gave the lady at the table my name and Willie's and picked up a map of the course.

"You're racing that dog?" she asked, leaning over the table to peer at Willie. "What's the matter with his eyes?"

I smiled at her. "Willie's blind," I said, "totally blind." And I took my map and walked out into the arena.

"No matter how it turns out," Cassie said, "you two are mighty brave for even trying this."

I looked at the map. The obstacles were numbered in the order we were supposed to do them in: "Great! The tunnel's first! That's our best one!" I figured that was a good omen.

We walked to Number Two, a low crossbar jump. "He can do this one, too," Cassie said.

"Hey, Gimpy. What do you think you're doing?" Colton stood by the first set of jumps: Fencer tugged his leash and growled at Willie.

"Checking out the course, same as you." I kept Willie on my left side, as far from Fencer as I could. He pulled toward the other dog, growling.

"What?" Colton jeered. He slapped his leg. "Oh, this is gonna be good! The gimp and his blind old mutt. What a riot!"

I glared at him, my hands shaking and my heart beating fast. "I know you hit Ginny and left her alone!" I blurted out.

Colton stepped closer to me. Anger poured off him like heat. "If you say one word about that to anybody, anybody, I will make you wish you hadn't been born. Got it, amigo?"

I swallowed. Cassie glared at Colton and pulled my sleeve, leading me away. I was shaking with anger, but at least I'd said something to him.

"Easy, cowboy," Cassie said. "Stay calm. You gotta focus on the course now."

I shook Colton's threat out of my head, but my hands were still tight fists and my nails dug into my palms.

Third was a hanging tire jump. Willie had gotten good at that. Next, the teeter-totter. No problem. Likewise, the pause table and the weave poles. I was feeling more confident all the time.

Last obstacle. "Oh no," I muttered. "The wall!"

It was about four feet tall, made of horizontal red and blue boards. It looked like the Great Wall of China to me, unclimbable.

"What do you think?" I asked. "Can he do it?"

Cassie looked it over. Willie sniffed along the bottom and peed on the corner. Cassie ran her hand along the face of the wall.

"Look at this," she said. "The middle board sticks out. If he gets a paw on it, he could use it as a toehold and scramble over the top."

I ran my hand over it. "Maybe he could. But maybe it's just too high." My heart sank in my chest. "Oh, Cass, what if he can't do it? Colton will never let me live it down; I can hear him crowing about it now, the gimp and the blind dog trying to beat him at the trials."

"Stop it, Jasper," Cassie said. She gave me a look like a steel-toed boot in the ribs.

But I couldn't stop. "It was a stupid idea. I'm gonna drop out." I started limping back to the sign-up table, kicking my dreams through the dust.

Chapter 22

Cassie caught hold of my shirt. "Oh no you're not! You can't drop out." She turned me around to face her. "Not after all our hard work. You and Willie are going to run the course, just like we've been practicing. It doesn't matter if you win. And it doesn't matter what Colton or anyone thinks; you just have to try."

The announcer's voice boomed over the loudspeaker: "Contestants clear the course. First round of the dog agility trials. Large dog class first."

I swallowed hard. "Yeah, all right," I heard my voice crack, barely a whisper. "We'll do it."

"Good man!" Cassie slapped me on the back. "And good dog, Willie. Go get 'em!"

Willie and I lined up with the four other "large-dog class" contestants. Colton and Fencer stood second in line.

Cassie gave me a thumbs-up and headed for the bleachers where she could get the best view of the whole course.

"This is it, Willie. This is my chance to beat Colton." I scratched his ears. "I believe in you."

"First contestant, Jamie Rothford and her dog, Skylark."

Jamie waved to the crowd. She looked about Mom's age, but Dad's size: big-boned and strong-built. Her dog looked to be pure German shepherd: sleek black and tan with a narrow head and perked-up ears.

The starting buzzer blared across the arena. Willie jumped at the noise and skittered in a circle on the end of his leash. "Easy, boy." I pulled him in close and knelt next to him.

In the arena, Jamie ran for the tunnel and Skylark dived through. They zipped around the course, Jamie running beside her dog, graceful, perfectly in sync. Skylark soared over the jumps and scampered up and down the teeter-totter. She was too fast at the weave-poles, though, and missed three. That would take off some points. She finished by flying over the high wall like some kind of super-dog. Jamie and Skylark strode out of the arena as the announcer gave their time and score.

"Uh oh, Willie!" I clutched his leash tight. "Looks like we've got more competition than just Colton and Fencer."

I didn't have much time to worry about Jamie and Skylark, though; Colton and Fencer were next.

Colton strutted to the entry gate, Fencer trotting beside him. The buzzer blared and Willie jumped again. Colton ran to the tunnel. Fencer disappeared into one end and sprang out the other. Colton sprinted between the obstacles, urging Fencer on. He flew. Nothing was too much for him.

He leaped over each jump, dodged through the weave-poles, shot through the tire, and hurdled over the wall. They finished in even better time than Jamie and Skylark and hadn't missed a thing!

My stomach knotted up. The other dogs were so young and lean and fast. I looked at my big old dog, his blind blue eyes, his graying whiskers. This was a big mistake!

Next thing I knew, our names rang out over the loudspeaker. My hands trembled as I unclipped his leash. Willie threw his head around, sniffing the air, smelling the crowd and the other dogs.

Buzzzzz! Willie jumped. "Come on, boy," I tried to keep my voice steady. He turned toward me and followed. We were off!

I ran to the end of the tunnel. "Come, Willie, through the tunnel! Through!" He ducked his head and went into the mouth of the nylon tunnel. I ran to the other end. He popped out. So far, so good!

We ran to the crossbar jump. We were doing it! Willie jumped when I said, "Jump!" and somehow made it over. His back feet hit the poles but didn't knock them down.

Next, the hanging tire. Willie put his front paws on the tire and climbed through. "Good boy! What a champ!" I urged him faster with my voice. Up the teeter-totter and down the other side, easy as pie! I grinned. My stomach unknotted. Excitement coursed through me.

He jumped onto the pause table when I tapped it and said "Up!" He sat perfectly still until I called him over to the weave poles. He dodged in and out, not missing a single pole: Perfect! I breathed fast and deep, my heart thumping with pride. Only one obstacle left: the wall.

"Come on, Willie! You can do it!" Cassie's voice came loud and clear across the field.

We ran for the wall. I slapped it with my hand, letting him hear where it was. "Over! Over!" Willie was galloping toward it. Fast. He skidded to a stop at the foot of the wall. I slapped it again.

"Over, Willie!" I gritted my teeth. I wanted this so much. "Come on, boy! You can do it!" He put his front paws on the boards and stood up tall on his hind legs. His chin reached the top of the wall. He jumped, heaving himself upward. His front paws scrambled for the top of the wall. My heart was in my mouth. He was doing it! If he could just get a toehold on the boards with his hind feet. . . .

Then Willie's hind legs slipped out from under him. He thudded back down. My heart sank. He struggled back to his feet and put his front paws on the wall again, heaving himself toward the top. But he fell back down again.

He was just too heavy. His old legs weren't strong enough. I couldn't bear to watch him anymore. He was trying so hard to do what I asked.

I grabbed his collar. "It's okay, Willie, that's enough. It's okay." I pulled him away from the wall and led him out of the arena. We hadn't completed the course. We were disqualified.

I brushed past Colton and Fencer.

"Thanks for the entertainment, kid! That was hilari-ous!" He laughed and slapped his thigh. "I can't believe you even ran that old dog against Fencer!"

I turned and glared at him. "At least we tried," I said through my gritted teeth. "Come on, Willie."

I didn't watch the last contestants, just clipped on Wil-lie's leash and led him away from the arena. I felt so stupid. Who enters a blind dog in agility trials? And me running around with my limp. What had I been thinking?

Chapter 23

A loudspeaker crackled as I left the arena: "May I have your attention please. . . ." The voice paused while a rumble of thunder rolled over the fairgrounds. The sky hung dark above us. "We're looking for a lost child."

"Ginny is six years old, blond hair, wearing a white flowered dress, last seen in the trailer parking area."

What was supposed to be the best day ever had quickly turned into the worst.

"Come on, Willie." I led him back past the bucking chutes and exercise corrals, to where we'd last seen Ginny. Cassie caught up with us. "Sorry about the race," she said. "You guys did great, though. Willie did great. Fencer is so much younger and, well, stronger."

"I know," I tried to smile. "I just wanted to beat Colton so bad!"

The sky was darkening, a summer storm rolling in from the west. Charcoal-gray thunderheads rose up on the horizon and raced toward the fairgrounds. Lightning forked down about a half mile away, over the outskirts of town. Lightning with no rain—wildfire weather!

Ginny was gone. The running board was empty. Deputy Kim was talking to Colton and Ketz, all of them standing in the dust, lightning flashing down on the hills behind them. This was my chance to tell them what Colton had done. I drew myself up tall as I could. My heart beat fast and hard.

Colton's pa's rig skidded into the parking lot. He slammed the truck cab door behind him and strode over. He towered over Colton by a head.

"Where's your sister?"

Cassie and Willie and I stood on the edge of the crowd that was piling up like the storm clouds on the horizon.

"She wanted to look at the horses, so I brought her down here to the corrals," Colton lied. "I turned around to say 'Hi' to Ketz and she took off." He looked to Ketz to confirm his story, but Ketz was gone. Colton was on his own.

Colton's pa looked his son up and down, his eyes slit narrow and his mouth thin and tight. He raised his hand a little, glanced at the deputy and dropped it. "Can't do nothing right, can you?" he snarled.

Sheriff Gonzales had pulled into the lot and walked over to Deputy Kim, who pointed at Colton. "This is the girl's brother. He was supposed to be watching her when she went missing."

"When did you see her last?" the sheriff asked Colton.

"Can't have been more than forty-five minutes, maybe an hour." Colton threw a desperate look at his pa. "I've been looking for her everywhere."

That was it. I stepped up. My heart thundered in my ears.

"He left her there a long time ago, before the barrel races this morning," I said.

Colton's eyes got big, like he couldn't believe I'd crossed him. His face flushed red and he clenched both fists. "What do you know about it?"

"Did you see them, Jasper?" Sheriff Gonzales asked me.

"Yeah, I heard him telling her to sit by the trailer until he came back." Colton glared daggers at me and I paused. But Cassie gave me a hidden thumbs-up and I continued on. "I heard him slap her. She was crying."

Colton's pa paced in front of his son. His face turned purple-ish and his lips curled back. Colton was lucky Gonzales and Kim were there. I didn't reckon he'd be so lucky later, especially if Ginny came to harm.

The sheriff turned to Kim. "Get on the radio and call it in to dispatch. Tell them we may need the Canine Unit out of Hood River and a couple more search teams."

"We've only got a few hours of good daylight left." The sheriff was talking to the crowd now. "We'll need volunteers to start the search until we get backup."

He scanned the hills and ridges that circled town. Lightning forked down out of the overhanging clouds. A few seconds later, thunder boomed. "The dry lightning is only going to make things more dangerous," Gonzales said. "Fire crews are already working on a couple burns to the east. We need to move fast."

"Would she have tried to walk home?" Deputy Kim asked Colton's pa.

"No telling," he said. "I hope not." He scowled at his son. I felt a twinge of sympathy for Colton, just a twinge.

"Volunteers?" Gonzales asked. A dozen men and women and kids, along with me and Cassie, raised our hands.

"All right," he said. "Kim, take a group and search the fairgrounds and barns. Check with Larry in the parking lot, in case he saw her leave with anyone. The rest of you, come with me. We'll divide into teams and cover the hills around the fairgrounds."

"I'll get Rowdy," Cassie said. "I can see further and cover more ground on horseback." She headed for the corrals.

Kim reminded us, "Grab some water and a flashlight and rope if you have it. This could be a long night. If we find her, I mean, *when* we find her, she'll be tired and thirsty and scared. She might even hide from us for fear of getting in trouble." She stabbed a look at Colton's father.

"We'll find her, Pa," Colton said. But he looked scared and uncertain. "Fencer is a great tracker, not just the best agility dog." He shot me a smug glance. "He'll find her."

"Come on, Willie," I led him to the running board where we'd left Ginny. "Remember Ginny? Remember how you made her feel better?" He ran his big black nose along the metal step. He looked up at me with his milky blind eyes like he knew what needed to be done.

"Find her, Willie, find her."

Chapter 24

Willie put his nose to the dusty ground and started off, away from the trailer. The others, including Colton and his pa, were still organizing themselves, breaking into groups and talking about which way to go. But not Willie. He seemed to know exactly where to go.

Cassie rode away from the fairgrounds, following a trail up between the hills. Willie and I followed. The fairgrounds faded away behind us and the country opened up. Deer and cattle trails wound between sagebrush and stands of junipers.

Willie kept right on going, steady as a train. I knew now that his nose worked extra-well since he couldn't see. Cassie rode up to the hilltops, scanned around, then came back to us, shaking her head. I followed Willie and listened to the thunder rolling over the rimrock. The other searchers fanned out over the hills, walking fast up the gullies and along the ridgetops.

A faint whiff of smoke floated under the clouds. I thought I saw a yellow fire glow in front of us, far off on the horizon. Wildfire moved fast, especially if the wind whipped it along. Clouds, wind, smoke, and darkness not far off; what a mess! I hollered "Ginny!" between thunderclaps.

The real search dogs wouldn't be here for hours. Fencer and Willie were the only dogs sniffing along Ginny's trail. I heard Colton yelling at Fencer to "Find her, find her," but when I looked back, the dog was all over the place, pulling Colton off the trail, trying to light out after every jackrabbit that hopped by. From the hilltops on either side of us, I heard searchers calling, "Ginny, Ginny!"

I put everyone else out of my mind and concentrated on the ground in front of us. Cassie rode beside us on a flat stretch of grassland, past the hills that circled the town.

"She's gone a long way for such a little kid," I said. "Why in the world would she walk so far? Ginny!"

Cassie looked out over the flatlands to Sutton Mountain rising in the south. "Well, she might be smarter than we think. She's actually headed for home, as the crow flies."

"We better find her soon." I stooped and ran my fingers over a big paw print in the dust. "Anything could get her out here; cougar, rattlesnake, or just falling and hurting herself. And those fires are blowing this way."

Cassie bent to look at the print. "Yeah, cougar," she confirmed. "We better find her before dark. Ginny!"

Willie led me along a deer trail over the crest of a hill. He seemed so sure of himself, pulling hard and steady on the leash. Cassie pulled Rowdy to a stop on the hilltop, twisting in the saddle to look all around. "Ginny!" Her voice carried through the smoky air.

In the fading light, Willie and I stumbled and slipped in the loose rock. My short leg ached and my eyes burned with dust and smoke. We trudged up to the hilltop where Cassie and Rowdy stood like a statue. I sank down onto a boulder to rest. Willie tugged at his leash to keep going.

"He sure seems to be on the trail." I rubbed Willie's ears. "He keeps his nose to the ground like he's following her scent. Good boy. Fencer's off chasing rabbits and you just keep tracking Ginny."

Cassie, Rowdy, and Willie and I made our way down the hill. I let Willie pull me onward, down the hill and up a draw full of jumbled rock and juniper. I heard three or four other searchers coming up the draw behind us, hollering for Ginny as they walked.

Suddenly, Willie stopped and nosed something stuck on a branch of bitterbrush. A scrap of white and pink cloth hung like a little flag in the fading light. Cassie swung down off Rowdy to stand beside me.

As I pulled the scrap off the bush, Colton and Fencer clattered through the shale behind us.

"What is it?" Colton panted when he saw us stopped there. Willie ignored Fencer as the other dog growled and strained toward him.

"A piece of Ginny's dress." I turned away. "Come on, Willie, find her."

Colton yelled over his shoulder, "Pa, I found a piece of her dress. She went this way."

"You found it?!" It came out before I could stop it. "Willie found it!" Fencer and Willie snarled and leapt for each other. I pulled Willie back, even though I felt like lunging at Colton myself.

Cassie grabbed me by my shirt, pulling me out of my anger and back to the present situation. "Jasper, Ginny's still out there. Lost." All of a sudden, the fight went out of me.

"You're right," I glared at Colton. I was still mad, but finding Ginny was more important than revenge. That could wait. "Let's go."

Colton and his pa went up a fork in the trail to the right. We went left. Willie had his nose to the ground again. He led us down along an old streambed, rugged with big rocks and tangles of dead juniper branches.

It was getting harder and harder to see. Besides the moonless night coming on, the smoke was thickening around us. I kept stopping to look at the fire. The flames were glowing on the hilltops, maybe a mile or two behind us, and coming closer.

I coughed into the thickening smoke. Cassie had tied her bandana up over her face like a bandit. I held my shirt cuff over my nose and mouth and worried about Willie. How could he even smell Ginny's trail through all this smoke?

"Good boy, Willie. Keep going."

While I stumbled and bumbled along, Willie kept moving steadily, nose to the ground, sure-footed and strong. What an amazing dog I had!

I only hoped we'd find Ginny before dark, before the fire caught up with us, before it was too late.

Chapter 25

The streambed we were hiking down gradually narrowed and the rock walls closed in. I bumped into Willie when he stopped at the mouth of a slot canyon. The gap between the rocks was about five or six feet wide, a jagged black opening into darkness.

Willie barked toward the opening and cocked his head at the returning echo. "All right, Willie. I get it." I stroked his head as he pulled at his leash. "You think she's in there."

"Why would she go into the canyon?" I wondered out loud.

"Might seem like a safe place to hide from the fire, or just to rest, if you're a scared little girl." Cassie swung down beside me, holding Rowdy's reins as we both peered into the canyon's narrow mouth.

"Looks like a death trap to me." I shook my head in dismay.

Cassie wrapped Rowdy's reins around a sturdy sage branch. "Let's go." She gave me a little nudge forward.

I was never too fond of tight spaces, and tight dark spaces were worse. Still, I followed my dog and Cassie followed me, her hand gripping the back of my shirt.

The rock walls closed in on us. I hooked Willie's leash over my belt so I could feel my way along the narrow passage. I was as blind as my dog. I ran my hands along each rough rock wall, taking small shuffling steps. The cut through the rocks was cool. At first.

As we felt our way along, thunder rumbled through the gap behind us. Smoke began to snake into my throat and down into my lungs. After about twenty feet, I crumpled over, coughing.

Cassie hauled me up and pushed me forward. Another ten feet and we squeezed through a bend in the passage. The walls opened up and we tumbled out into the body of the canyon, first Willie, then me, then Cassie in a heap. The sky spread out above us, hazy through the smoke and gathering darkness. My breath came easier, but my eyes still stung as Cassie and I sat panting in the dirt.

On the rim above us, I could hear the fire whoosh and suck as the east wind kicked it closer. Sagebrush crackled and junipers exploded. I watched a flaming branch tumble down the far canyon wall. Some small creature, probably a cottontail, bumped my boot on its way out the canyon mouth, away from the fire.

The air got hotter and hotter. Cassie and I held our hands over our faces. How could Willie smell anything in this? Other animals crashed by us, deer, ground birds flapping and screeching. Flaming tumbleweeds rolled down like fireballs from the canyon rim.

"We don't know if she's even in there, Jasper," Cassie shouted over the cracking and crackling and whooshing of the fire. "The fire's coming on too fast. We could get trapped. We should head back."

Willie pulled hard on his leash, tugging us deeper into the canyon.

Cassie stopped behind us. "What if he's not on her trail at all, Jasper?" She had to shout over the crackling fire.

"No." I wouldn't quit now. "Willie knows she's in there. I trust him!"

We pushed on. Cassie followed.

Willie nosed into a thick pile of broken sage and tumbleweeds. He came back out and barked, like he had discovered something important. Then he shouldered his way deeper into the pile. Cassie and I pulled the dry bushes away. It looked like a brushy nest in the rocks, a perfect hiding spot. But if the flames caught it, we were all goners.

I heard a whimper, like a rabbit in a snare. We had dug into the brush four feet or so when Willie backed out dragging Ginny by her dress like a limp doll. Cassie and I grabbed her arms and pulled her the rest of the way free. She was scratched up and dirty and her Sunday shoes were gone.

She coughed and hacked as I hefted her in my arms, carrying her back the way we'd come, toward the cleft entrance of the canyon. I didn't feel her weight at all; she was like an angel fallen against my shoulder. Willie stumbled behind us.

I said over and over, "Good boy, Willie. Good dog." Smoke-flavored tears ran down my face. I could hardly believe what my old blind dog had done.

Sheriff Gonzales met us as we fell out of the slot canyon into the open. He lifted Ginny from my arms and someone pushed a bottle of water into my hand. My worn-out legs shook.

Colton and his dad raced up. They didn't say anything to us, but grabbed Ginny and hugged her and carried her off. The fire crept around the canyon rim toward us.

"Come on," Gonzales pulled Cassie and me away from the canyon mouth. "The fire's closing in fast." I turned back. Where was Willie? He wasn't walking beside me anymore. When had I dropped his leash?

Then I saw him, a darker heap in the darkness, just outside the canyon entrance. I sprinted back and dropped down next to him, taking his big head into my lap. His breath was shallow on my hand.

Willie wasn't moving. He was barely breathing, his chest nearly still.

Oh, God, I thought, my dog! My good, brave dog! The race wore him out, then all the smoke, the long, rough trail. What had I done to him? Was he going to die on me now, after all we'd been through together?

Cassie knelt beside us. She cupped her hands around Willie's snout and blew air into his nose and mouth. Nothing.

Chapter 26

I stroked Willie's side, feeling for a heartbeat, a breath, while Cassie puffed air into his nose and mouth again, drew a breath herself then blew again.

"Give him a little water," she panted.

I dripped some water onto his tongue when she leaned back to get her breath. I felt his chest again. Only the slightest movement.

"Come on, Willie, *breathe*," I begged. "Don't leave me!"

Suddenly, Willie coughed, then sneezed, then raised his head.

"Oh, good boy! Good boy!" I hugged him tight around the neck. "You did it, Cassie! You saved him!"

Willie looked up at me with his blind eyes and smiled his toothy grin, like he'd only been fooling with us. Cassie hugged him, too.

Willie struggled to stand, but his legs buckled and he sank to the ground.

"He can't walk all the way back to town," I said. "What are we going to do?"

"Rowdy can carry him if he lies still." She led her horse

over and together we lifted the big dog up and laid him across the saddle. Rowdy turned and sniffed Willie, but didn't fuss.

Cassie led Rowdy while I walked alongside, steadying Willie.

As we stumbled slowly down through the growing darkness, fire crews with shovels and hard hats passed us going toward the flames. A helicopter with a bag of pond water slung under it chuffed over us.

Cassie and I staggered into town. Someone had a hose running where the other searchers sat or lay on the soft green courthouse lawn like fallen statues from a war. We doused our heads and scrubbed our arms. Willie sank onto his stomach, his head between his paws.

Colton and his family were there too. A crowd was gathered around Ginny; I could just barely see her sitting on the tailgate of the sheriff's truck, wrapped in a green blanket. Deputy Kim was holding her wrist and looking at her watch, checking her pulse.

Colton left his dad and Ginny talking to the sheriff and came over to us. He looked me straight in the eye and reached out his hand. I was surprised, but I took it and we shook.

"Thanks," he said quietly. There was no anger in his voice, no sarcasm. Next he thanked Cassie and laid a hand on Willie's head. Colton shuffled his feet and dropped his eyes. "Sorry, Jasper," he said quietly. "Really, I'm sorry." Without another word he turned and walked back to his sister.

Colton lifted Ginny from their father's arms and held her against his chest. She rested her dirty cheek on his shoulder. Fencer whined, tied to the bumper of the sheriff's truck.

Cassie and I sat petting Willie where we'd laid him on the grass. He was breathing easier now, his ribcage rising and falling, but his eyes were closed. He must have been exhausted. Sheriff Gonzales, Deputy Kim, and a handful of others walked over to where we sat.

"You two are heroes," Gonzales said as he reached out and shook my hand, then Cassie's. "Good job."

"No, sir," I said, shaking my head, "Willie's the hero." I ran a hand over my dog's head. He sat up and wagged his tail.

The sheriff petted him and held the dog's chin up, looking into Willie's sightless eyes. "Yep, that's some great dog you have here, Jasper. You take good care of him. We may need him again someday."

"Oh yeah." I smiled and hugged Willie. "Don't worry about that; I'll look after him."

Deputy Kim and some of the others who'd been out searching came over to pet Willie. Someone even brought him a hot dog, his favorite snack! They fawned over him and he sat up tall and thumped his tail against the ground.

My parents drove up with Cassie's dad's truck right behind them. After they got the story from Deputy Kim, we got hugged and congratulated until my legs nearly collapsed from tiredness.

Mom put her arm around my shoulder. "Let's get home," she said.

"Bye, Cass." I waved at her. "Thanks, amigo."

"So long, Cowboy." Cassie grinned at me. She swung up on her horse. "Bye, Willie."

"Sure am proud of you, son," Dad said as I hoisted Willie onto the seat and squeezed in beside him. I was pretty proud of us, too.

Willie woofed and licked my face. After all his heroics, I think he was glad to be going home.

Epilogue

Sheriff Gonzales called me twice that summer, asking Willie and me to help on search-and-rescue crews. One time, we helped track a toddler who'd wandered away from the family's ranch. Willie tracked him down to an old barn on a deserted farm nearby.

The second time, we searched for some deer hunters who'd driven up from the city and didn't come back to their camp that night. The next morning, Willie led a group of us from their truck into the sagebrush hills. We finally heard them yelling from a cave where they'd spent the night.

Willie became a local celebrity: the rescue crews loved him and his amazing nose. He never got much better at the agility course, but it didn't matter to either of us. We had a more important job to do and we were good at it.

Colton still gave me a hard time in front of his friends, but he never beat me up again. And while I still had my limp, I sure walked a little taller after that summer. Willie never could see with his eyes, but always he saw with his heart. I knew for sure that we'd done the right thing that day at the shelter when we chose each other.

Jasper and Willie: Wildfire
Study Guide Questions

1. Why do you think Colton bullies Jasper? Have you ever been picked on or bullied? Have you bullied someone else?

2. How does Cassie's friendship help Jasper achieve his goals?

3. Jasper gets braver as he faces his fears: What have you done that scared you? How did you feel afterward?

4. Jasper works hard to get his dog. What would you do to get something you wanted badly? What would you give up?

5. How does Willie's blindness make him a good search dog?

6. Jasper, Cassie, and Willie worked together to save the lost girl. What did each of them contribute to the search? Could any of them have done it without the others?

31901056789748

CPSIA information can be obtained at www.ICGtesting.com
Printed in the USA
BVOW08s0237100715

407416BV00001B/1/P

9 781941 821718